SUNRISE DREAMS

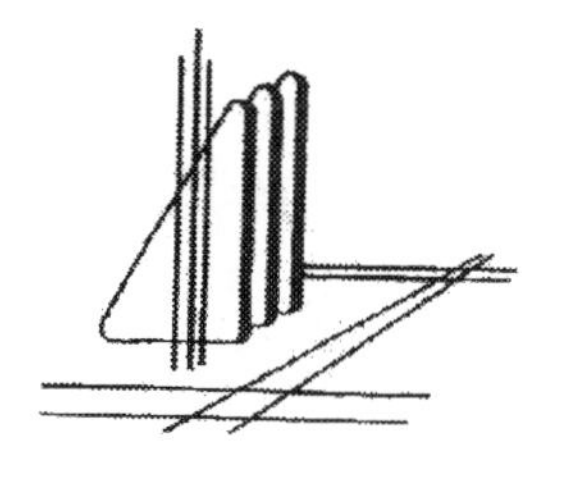

SUNRISE DREAMS

Giving Our Best Dreams Their Best Chance to Happen

Don C. Davis, ThB, BA, MDiv

Archway Publishing books may be ordered through booksellers or by contacting:

Archway Publishing
1663 Liberty Drive
Bloomington, IN 47403
www.archwaypublishing.com
1-(888)-242-5904

Cover inspiration by Nolan Davis

ISBN: 978-1-4808-1597-1 (e)
ISBN: 978-1-4808-1598-8 (sc)
ISBN: 978-1-4808-1596-4 (hc)

Library of Congress Control Number: 2015902744

Print information available on the last page.

Archway Publishing rev. date: 3/10/2015

ACKNOWLEDGEMENTS

A Place in the Story is the best of positive future-vision fiction, inspired by successful achievers.

Inspiration for my novel in seven sequels, *A Place in the Story*, has come from multiple sources, but none greater than from my wife, Mary, and our sons, Charles and Nolan, and their families. Mary, whose own success story continues to inspire her family, has been my devoted supporter and skillful editor. Along with these, there is the continuing influence of having loving parents who were good people.

The overview nature of my books has come from a list of writers whose books and articles explored the future, advanced knowledge, shared their knowledge base from science and technology, inspired positive insights, and led the way to a knowledge-based faith.

Those who have had a major influence on my thoughts and paradigms include: Norman Vincent Peale, Napoleon Hill, Albert Schweitzer, Og Mandino, Carl Sagan, Norman Cousins, Bill Gates, Fulton Oursler, Dale Carnegie, Theodore Gray, Norman Doidge, Martin E. P. Seligman, Michio Kaku, and others, whose vision is a reference to the future more than to the past.

From these, I have gathered an overarching view of the future. Like an impressionist painting, these provide a bigger picture of our place in the story for new tomorrows and the new sacred.

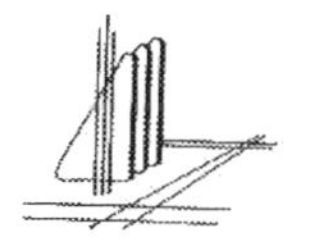

Chapter One

MEMORIAL TRIBUTE To Dr. JAMES KELLY

"All any of us ever get is a place in the story."

The final days for Dr. James Kelly were filled with a hope that his family, especially all his grandchildren, would be at his memorial service at the church near the farmhouse where he had grown up.

After the minister at New Home Church had led the service up to the time for a memorial tribute to be given by the family, Steve walked slowly from his pew to the chancel and stood behind the old pulpit his granddad had stood behind as a boy and dreamed of the future. That old dark pulpit had been saved when the white wood frame church of his boyhood days had been torn away and replaced with a new brick structure. To have the usual pulpit set aside temporarily and the old pulpit placed in the chancel during his memorial service was a part of Dr. Kelly's request.

Steve looked down at his family, took a deep breath, and began tenderly. "Our gathering here today is in respectful tribute to the life of Dr. James Kelly. Soon after our much loved granddad died, Grandmother said to me, 'Steve, you and your granddad were very close. I know how much you admired him and how very much he admired and trusted you. You've got to speak for all of us at his memorial service.' I am honored to fulfill that request. In great respect for the partnership that Grandmother and Granddad shared for fifty-six years, I speak for all the family in a tribute of honor and great admiration.

All any of us ever get is a place in the story. That was one of Granddad's often repeated phrases. Granddad's place in the story has been one of great honor, high respect, and distinguished nobility. Dr. James Kelly was held in high esteem by all who knew him - by his whole family, by all those who were privileged to listen to his sermons, by those who listened to his common sense philosophy in his classrooms, and by those who heard him speak at major conferences. He was held in high esteem by all of us. To have known him personally, is to remember him as a kind and caring person, a practical, honorable philosopher, and distinguished gentleman. What made him stand so tall among all of us was the magnitude of his mind, his intellectual integrity, and his warm and caring congeniality.

Front and center in Dr. Kelly's own story, he wanted to be remembered as a person who envisioned a future based in the Big Ten Universal Qualities that can be lived out in the everyday lives of all the world's people, as world citizens, wherever their journey story takes place."

Steve paused and looked down a moment, before he looked up again and said, tearfully, "I can't stand here behind this old pulpit, where Granddad stood as a boy and dreamed of his future, without shedding tears. So give me a moment." After wiping away his tears, Steve said, "Not only has Grandmother asked me to speak, but Granddad had also asked me to speak at his memorial service.

Not long before Granddad's closing days, he was one of the speakers at the World Future Conference. He asked me to go with him to that conference where distinguished leaders from around the world gather to think ahead about the progression of the human story. I was honored to be asked to be there and to hear his presentation which summarized his faith and philosophy of life.

While we were at that conference, he talked about having more days behind him than before him. I had never heard him speak in that manner before. He talked about his memorial service and asked me to speak. 'I have a special request,' he said. 'I want you to include some of what I will say at this conference.' I had a copy of his manuscript, but as he spoke, I listened with more than usual attention.

What he said in his presentation to that distinguished world audience was a basic statement of his personal philosophy of life and future vision. It was the magnitude of his thoughts that led him to venture into new frontiers of vision. In deep respect, I want to share selected excerpts from that visionary presentation.

It bore the appropriate title, "THE NEW SACRED." He began with three questions, First, he asked, 'What if one of the most important uphill challenges of our time is to make sure the qualities of our humanity keep up with, even lead, our science and technology?' Then, second, he asked, 'What if we had ten universal qualities which are so rewarding they could be used as word tools to define a new sacred for our world family as the future we ask for?' His third question was, 'What if we learn as much as we can about how all molecular existence works, and learn how to work with the way it works, so that we dare to dream bold new dreams for the human family far down into distant tomorrows, and give those dreams their best chance to happen?'

He answered his own questions in the thesis he presented at the World Future Conference. He said, 'In the progression of our human story, as a sweeping collective identity, we are moving away from transcendence to immanence, from a vertical viewpoint to a horizontal paradigm. We are crossing a great divide from authority-based religion, informed by persistent old world views in mythology, tradition, and literalized sacred texts, over to a knowledge-based faith, informed by science, technology, and the Big Ten Universal Qualities as a guiding template we can overlay on our identity to guide us to the greatest future ever dreamed.

This knowledge-based faith is so basic and overarching that, when it guides what we plan to give to life, it becomes a sacred request of life. It's a faith that respects the oneness of all molecular existence and our place in that mysterious and amazing story. What we are learning is, that the story of our existence is an ongoing fantastic story in which everything is interrelated, even how we are learning about the oneness of all existence is that even plants are aware of other nearby plants, and act in interrelated concert. Even how we think about this interconnectedness is itself a part of this overall oneness. We are a part of all that is and it is a part of us. However remote and infinitesimally small, there is a collective nature of our place in all things that becomes a kind of total environment. Learning how to respect that is the new sacred.'

Granddad believed some universal qualities have come into focus in our time that can help us define and shape our tomorrows that are far better than our yesterdays. He said, 'We have not lived up to our potential. We can do better! I believe there are now ten universal qualities that can lead the way to a great new age of promise.'

Our respected and admired Dr. James Kelly lived by those qualities. If we want to know what kindness and caring look like, we can see them in the story of Dr. James Kelly. Perfect? No. But we all know he was always reaching for his best. If he failed, he didn't stop there. He learned from his failures and kept on reaching. That un-relinquished quest became a part of his diplomacy and his nobility, and we all loved him for it.

As an integral part of his thesis, he asked pointedly, 'What are the Big Ten Universal Qualities which can shape our best future?' Then one by one, he recounted those world citizen qualities: *'KINDNESS, CARING, HONESTY, RESPECT, COLLABORATION, TOLERANCE, FAIRNESS, INTEGRITY, DIPLOMACY, NOBILITY'*

These Big Ten identity markers are so basic, so healthy, so wholesome, and so rewarding that they add an important compliment to any religion, all politics, and varying cultures. They can be chosen by anyone, anywhere, anytime as an identity framework which respects our place in the oneness of all existence. They can guide the human family to the greatest era of common good the world has ever known. These words are at the heart of the new sacred.'

As I was preparing for this memorial tribute, I read from my copy of the presentation Dr. Kelly made to that distinguished audience, and decided that I could do no better than to share some more of his presentation, as a tribute of honor to his life and story. To that world audience, he told a simple story from his early country life that showed the progression of knowledge he respected so highly.

He said, 'One fall evening in my boyhood days, when the air was chilly, the persimmons were orange, the pumpkins were yellow, and red, yellow, and brown leaves were falling from the trees, I walked a half mile down the dusty country road to be a part of a neighborhood corn shucking. When I got there, the farmer had already gathered the corn and had it lying on the ground in a long pile. For many days, the farmer had taken his mules and wagon out to the corn field and had picked the ears of corn off the stalk one by one, thrown them into the wagon, and hauled them to the barnyard where he unloaded them out of the wagon onto the ground in a long pile. I joined others who sat on the ground and reached for the ears of corn, pulled the shucks off, tossed the shucks behind us, and pitched the corn across the old pile into a new pile.

There was a legend that if a boy found a red ear of corn, he got to kiss any girl of his choice. I struck out on both counts. I never did find a red ear of corn. And, as a ten year old country boy, there was no girl anywhere that I wanted to kiss. That changed when I got to college. I still hadn't found a red ear of corn, but I did find a girl I wanted to kiss, and I kissed her, and married her, several years ago.'

All of us here today know that person was our beloved Maria, mother, grandmother, teacher, friend, and distinguished lady. Granddad said that he always had to live up to her. What we sense is that they lived up to each other with great respect.

Granddad bridged his barnyard corn shucking story over into a technological version of corn shucking. With obvious excitement about the advances in technology, he said, 'Recently, I was driving out to the farm when I met a John Deere combine coming toward me, taking up the full width of the road. What did I do? I pulled off onto the shoulder of the road and stopped, and let that technological monster have the right of way! You would have, too! It had four giant tires on the front, two on each side, as tall as I, and two, only slightly smaller tires, on the back that would swivel so that big combine could turn. High up in the center of that commanding unit, a farmer was sitting in a glassed-in, air-conditioned cab, driving that modern day corn shucker. That's the kind of unit that pulls up on a seven acre cornfield near the barn and harvests that entire field in just over seventy minutes. It not only picks the corn, but shucks it, shells it, then augers it over into a big truck, waiting to take it to a storage unit. Now that's the way to shuck corn!'

But Granddad's story of our earth family's progression did not stop there. He said, 'That progression in corn shucking is but one example of the ways we have combined mind and hand to create the tools of technology that provide so many wonderful things that have expanded the horizons of human achievement. In our digital-information-molecular age, we have created the electron microscope and the large Hadron Collidor that take us to the micro edge of our atomic world. At the other extreme, we have built the Hubble Telescope, and are building its successor, the Kepler Telescope, to take us to the macro edge of our universe. We have created the internet and cell phones to connect us together in a global oneness as the human family on our planet. Out of our growing collective knowledge, we have collaborated as a tremendous search team and created the robotic space explorer, Curiosity, to extend our venture in knowledge about our place in the story out into the edge of our solar system, and it's place in limitless space. There, one hundred and forty-seven million miles from its planet home, this complex robotic creation now represents us on Mars in a quest for understanding who we are in the scope and nature of molecular existence beyond our earth home.'

Then, very intentionally, he said, 'All this brings us face to face with a new challenge, to make sure our technology and our humanity go hand in hand to lead our story to the next level up to where we give our best dreams their best chance to happen. It's here, on our planet now that we are among the most privileged people in all of the human story. It's here we can choose the Big Ten Universal Qualities as an identity template we can live by so our humanity can parallel, even lead, our technology.'

Dr. Kelly talked about the importance of our tools. He said, 'In our successive ages, it is the progression of our tools that has made such a difference in our sixty-five thousand years of human story – at first, hand tools made from the sticks and stones of nature, then hand crafted tools, then machine tools, then digital tools, then nano scale tools. But, now the most important tools that we have to advance us forward in our John Deere age are our word tools – words that respect how the world works and how we can work with how the world works so that we build a better world by becoming better people.'

Granddad believed the word tools of the Big Ten Universal Qualities will be of immense importance for the forward progress of our story for many generations into the future. I listened to Granddad when he spoke to that world audience. He said, 'So, I have a dream, that the Big Ten Universal Qualities can be incorporated into all the world family's learning centers! These qualities can be taught. They can be learned as a healthy, wholesome, rewards-based identity! They can be embraced by any person, anywhere, anytime, on location, in residence, to define the promise of the future in terms of how we can define our highest humanity! The marvel is that we not only get to glimpse that kind of future but, in this pivotal age, we can be engaged in those causes which advance the progress of humanity's sunrise dreams. We can shape our future. That, my colleagues, is sacred!'

Dr. James Kelly's lifetime of ministry, which began with boyhood dreams behind this old pulpit, has been a ministry to the mind, with a noble vision for a future, defined by the Big Ten Universal Qualities. That visionary leader, who shared his dream on a world stage, is the person we salute today for the magnitude of his mind, the vision in his dreams, and the nobility of the qualities he lived out.

If I stop here, I will not have shared the full scope of his vision that he shared with that world audience. He wanted to show how his Big Ten paradigm squared with the leading edge of the schools of knowledge, and great humanitarian causes. So, as part of our respectful salute to this stalwart world citizen, let me share more of his presentation.

He said, 'The identity defined by the Big Ten Universal Qualities, aligns with a molecular and neuroscience understanding of who we are, as defined in Norman Doidge's book, *The Brain that Changes Itself* - that the brain is plastic and programmable - that it can rewrite some of its own software, especially when we are children and youth, but also down into senior years, where the signals we input to the brain can be our identity GPS to guide us to a great new era of qualities-based living and great new possibilities!

This Big Ten identity framework aligns with the positive psychology that Martin E. P. Seligman, former president of the American Psychological Association, sets forth in his book,

Authentic Happiness. The focus for this leading psychologist is on self-development and personal strengths which increase the positive guiding expectations we set for ourselves.

A Big Ten identity aligns with how Ted Turner framed his answer to the question when he was asked, 'What do we need for America to be great?' He said, 'What we need is for humanity to be great!'

When we choose to live by a Big Ten identity that helps us align with the premise of the Bill and Melinda Gates Foundation, that all people deserve to live a healthy life.

This human qualities identity that we can choose for our place in the story, aligns with the Clinton Global Initiative, where the goal is to work together to forge solutions to the world's most pressing challenges.

If enough people choose to live by the Big Ten Universal Qualities, these defining qualities will guide the human family to a new version of, one small step for man; one giant leap for mankind, not on the moon, but here on earth where we can be world citizens. That is the new sacred!

So, I have a dream,' Granddad said as he continued in his own Martin Luther King oratorical style, and repeating what he had said earlier about teaching the Big Ten Universal Qualities, 'I have a dream that the Big Ten Universal Qualities can be incorporated into all the world family's learning centers and identity paradigms! I have a dream that these qualities can be taught and learned as a framework for a healthy rewards-based identity, and when embraced by any person, anywhere, anytime, on location, will lead to a greater future!'

He said, 'My dream for our future aligns with the proverb of Solomon, "Teach a child to choose the right path, and when he is older he will remain upon it."' (*Proverbs 22:6 TLB)*

I was listening intently and respectfully when Granddad paused briefly, dropped his voice into an even more serious tone, and said, 'In our time, some say we have an education deficit. But that's not all. What we have is an identity deficit. It is a deficit in learning the universal qualities, not only in our families, but in all our schools and religious education programs for the children and youth, at the time when the brain is most ready to develop a dependable identity GPS to guide them to their best life.'

Slowing his words even more to a very deliberate statement, Granddad said, 'No boy or girl, who grows up in any of our learning centers at home, church, or school, should ever have to say, "I never was taught the Big Ten Universal Qualities." These quality markers are so important, and so basic, they belong right along with learning the ABCs, the multiplication table, and the periodic table of the one hundred and eighteen elements of all known molecular existence. Having the Big Ten identity markers as part of each child's healthy identity GPS is more important now than at any other time in all human history.'

He continued thoughtfully, 'The identity deficit is serious, but solvable! We have an immediate opportunity to teach these as guiding identity markers in all our teaching-learning settings. As parents, teachers, and public leaders, we can make these valuable guiding markers the flagship words we choose to define who we are trying to be as world citizens in the greatest age we have ever known! That is the new sacred.'

Granddad dropped his head and paused a moment. Then he looked up and said slowly, 'I know I will never live to see the teaching part of my dream completed. That's why it is important to launch a new Big Ten Generation as carriers of this dream. We are in need of new pioneering visionaries who will take these guiding markers to the next level up in all the learning channels of the human family.'

Granddad paused again and looked upward as though he were seeing a vision of the future. His tone of voice indicated that he was at the end of his presentation. He said, 'I don't know what the future will be like, or even what it can be like, but I am sure of this - that it is better to reach for our best dreams, even if we never achieve them fully, than never to have dreamed at all! It's time to make shaping the future of our human story into a Big Ten request of life. That is as sacred as it gets!'

Granddad paused again and looked upward as though he were seeing a vision of the future. His tone of voice indicated he was near the end of his presentation. He said, 'I don't know what the future will be like, or even what it can be like, but I am sure of this – that it is better to reach for our best dreams, even if we never achieve them fully, than never to have dreamed at all. It is time to shape the future of our human story by a Big Ten request of life. That's the new sacred we can carry forward across the generations.

We can frame our vision in the words of the prophet Joel, *"Your sons and daughters shall prophesy, and your young men shall see visions, and your old men shall dream dreams." Acts 2:17 KJV*

'That's us! Young and old, we are those sons and daughters who prophesy, see visions, and dream dreams. We need a new Big Ten Generation who will take up the unfinished dream of the Master Teacher to build a kingdom of heaven on earth as only we can build it with a knowledge-based faith where we put our science, technology, and the Big Ten Universal Qualities together as on-going sunrise dreams!'

Steve waited until he could transition from sounding almost like his granddad speaking. He said, "Dr. James Kelly was a highly respected and esteemed minister, a professor and philosopher admired by hundreds of students, acclaimed speaker, devoted marriage partner, loving parent and grandparent, and friend to all of us. Our tribute to him reflects the magnitude of his mind, the generosity of his friendship, and the nobility of his dreams. Granddad had an aura about him that was warm and caring. We sensed that he loved us. And, all of us loved him!

Yesterday morning as I walked along beside the shrubbery at the farmhouse, I heard a high pitched humming sound. I thought it must be the bees on the shrubbery. But, no, there were no bees on the shrubbery. Then I looked at the soyzia grass that covers the entire lawn. It was in full bloom and bees were going from tiny flower to tiny flower, gathering nectar. That was the high pitched humming sound I heard. It was not the sound of one bee, or hundreds, but of thousands collecting honey together by doing what each bee can do, one, by one, by one.

That's the way of Granddad's vision. He wanted the humming sound of the words of the Big Ten Universal Qualities to be heard across the world to define an identity and a future for the human family that is not just newer, or longer, but better. He echoed the hope of Abraham Lincoln, that we would develop 'the better angels of our nature.'

Dr. James Kelly earned the right to be called a world citizen. He lived out those qualities which anyone, anywhere, at anytime can choose to define their place in the world family and its best new tomorrows. With distinction and nobility, he commanded respect and stood tall among men of all time.

One of the ways we can honor him here at his memorial service is to take up the torch that has now been passed down to us. It's almost like we can hear him now, quoting James Weldon Johnson's poem:

> *Sing a song full of the faith that the dark past has taught us;*
> *sing a song full of the hope that the present has brought us;*
> *facing the rising sun of our new day begun,*
> *let us march on till victory is won.*

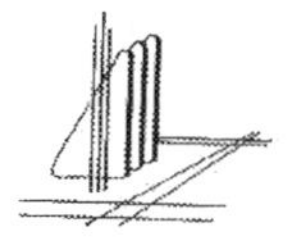

Chapter Two

On the Porch Again

'What you need to do is to get the Big Ten words into stories.'

FOLLOWING THE MEMORIAL SERVICE, FRIENDS AND FAMILY GATHERED at the farmhouse. It was as Granddad had said, 'My memorial service must be at my boyhood church and afterwards you must gather at the farmhouse where I grew up, and where the family has shared so many wonderful times together. Then chart new tomorrows. Life must go on.'

Back at the farmhouse, Grandmother put her arms around Steve's shoulder and said, "Steve, you were masterful in representing all of us at the service. It was so right to include much of what your granddad said at the World Future Conference, as your tribute. It represented him and who he was. You know this already, but it was your granddad's wish that his grandchildren gather on the porch after the memorial service to extend the story seminar which was such a crowning moment for him. He often spoke of that high privilege he had of telling his future vision stories to all of you grandchildren. Those stories were reflections out of yesterday, but they shined a light on new tomorrows. It's like he kept on saying, 'All of us must keep on turning old endings into new beginnings. The future must always be more important than the past. After all, life moves on, and all any of us ever get is a place in the story.' So, Steve, while all of you are here, could all of you gather on the porch again, and could you take your place in his chair and lead the new story seminar?"

"Grandmother," Steve said, holding back to keep his voice from breaking, "Sitting in his chair will not be easy, but it will be a high honor."

One by one, Steve asked his cousins to gather on the porch. As he approached the chair at the bend of the wraparound porch where Granddad had sat to tell the stories, which were later published as his book, *New Tomorrows,* he paused and looked down at the chair in respectful memory, then sat down. After another pause, he began reflectively. "Can you imagine how it feels to sit here where I was asked to sit? I had rather any of you were sitting here. But upon Grandmother's request, I will not only take the seat, but do so in great respect for the legacy Granddad left to all of us.

As all of us sit here on the Kudzu lined porch, we are a part of the legacy and request Granddad made near the end of his life. Somehow he sensed that his days were few. He said, 'Steve, I want all of you to meet on the porch again, after my memorial service, and take up the questions I posed when I spoke at the World Future Society Conference.'

I know I am repeating some of what I said at Granddad's memorial service, but we do well to recall the word tools Granddad used to define a higher humanity and a better world: Kindness, Caring, Honesty, Respect, Collaboration, Tolerance, Fairness, Integrity, Diplomacy, Nobility. Those words recur again and again in his writings and in his story telling. The repetition was intentional so they would become implanted in the mind. And we know those words do not stand alone. They are defining words to build a partnership in which science and technology and universal qualities go hand in hand to form a knowledge- based faith as a new sacred.

Granddad wanted me to go with him to the World Future

Conference. When we were at the opening reception, Granddad and I sat down at a table and began talking with one of the persons who was influential in founding the World Future Society. I watched as Granddad handed him one of his business cards on which the Big Ten Universal Qualities were listed. He looked them over quietly, then looked up at Granddad and said, 'What you need to do is to get the Big Ten words into stories.' What I knew, and what Granddad knew, but in his modesty did not tell him, was that he had already done that. And what we know, as we sit here on the porch again, is that we were the ones who were privileged to hear those words in his stories before they were published.

When Granddad made his presentation to that world audience of distinguished leaders, at one point he asked this pointed question, 'What about our humanity - who do we want to be?'"

Steve took a deep breath and leaned back a little more and said, "I am assuming that is the question Granddad wanted us to reflect upon and the reason he wanted us to meet here on the porch again. He said to me, 'Steve, there is a part of my story that remains unfulfilled. It's that part of a dream where the Big Ten Universal Qualities are taught to the children of the whole world as ten overarching and defining words that can be chosen to guide them and the human family to great new tomorrows.'

Addressing me quite intentionally, as though he expected me to pass the torch on, he said, 'You and your cousins must help me fulfill that part of my unfulfilled dream. I never did get the Big Ten Universal Qualities launched into the teaching-learning centers the way they need to be. These universal qualities need to be taught to children, especially to middle school children. My failure at that point is your opportunity. I want my grandchildren to take the teaching of these important identity markers to the next level. It's a dream on a scale of millions, but it must happen on a scale of one. For that to happen, these words must be taught so that, one by one, they will be learned as ten overarching identity markers to guide one's place in the story.'"

Grandmother appeared, but had stood waiting and listening until Steve completed Granddad's memorable charge. When she stepped forward with her plate of cookies and pitcher of tea, Steve said, "Grandmother! You didn't forget! You always kept us supplied with tea and cookies. How special that you should appear now at this special moment when we need, not only the tea and cookies, but the inspiration you have always added. We are searching for answers to Granddad's question about our humanity - about who we want to be. The challenge he left with us is to find ways the Big Ten can be taught. So, Grandmother, you are a teacher, help us out. What must we do now?"

Grandmother set the tea and cookies down on the table and answered, almost quizzically. "That's a mighty short question to such an important challenge. But, here's my short answer. I know what your Granddad did, and what I have done as a teacher, along with him, across all these years. We told stories. So that's my answer. Tell stories. Stories are the best carriers of vision and paradigms. Get your ideas into stories. Tell your own stories which explore identity options. Now help yourself to tea and cookies. You'll need an extra burst of energy to come up with your own good stories."

As she turned to leave, they all stood and spoke in an array of expressions, "Thank you, Grandmother, for the cookies and tea, but especially for being such a wonderful grandmother."

When they sat down again, Steve picked up on her advice about telling stories and said, summarizing her advice, "Tell stories. That's the same answer one of the leaders at the World Future Society gave when Granddad talked with him at a reception, he said, 'Get the Big Ten words into stories.'"

"They are both so right," Marsha said immediately. "Granddad inserted his ideas and paradigms about who we are into stories and extended their meaning into new times for new generations. He was an artist in telling stories. An artist captures a moment in history but then extends its impact as metaphors far beyond that, even up to the present and future. Granddad did that. He liked to search for the big picture and extended meanings."

Marsha turned to Linda and said, "Linda, I am an artist. I see the art in Granddad's storytelling, but you are a teacher. How do you see how all this applies to us, especially in terms of teaching? Can you give us a lead?"

"A lead?" Linda said, a bit startled at the request, but with a ready answer, she said, "I don't know of one better than the one Grandmother has just given to us. Tell stories. But she also said for us to tell our own stories. What if we did that now and each of us told a story? What if each of us chose one of the Big Ten Universal Qualities and told how it is, or can be, a story related to our careers? Could we all do that now? What do you think, Steve?"

"What I think," Steve said, "that is a great idea. So, Linda, maybe you could continue."

Linda responded immediately. "If I get to choose a word it will be **Collaboration**. It's what Granddad did in many ways. It has to do with working together. And working together is what I try to teach children. We even work in teams to incorporate collaboration into experience. Collaboration has never been more important than it is now. We need it in our families and in our family of nations. We need it in our work and careers. But we need it personally. Children need to learn collaboration in school. And since teaching is what I do, I can even share some ideas, if you are interested." She looked from side to side at her cousins to assess their interest.

"I think you have a, 'go' on that offer," Steve said. "I think we are all deeply interested."

Linda proceeded with enthusiasm. "In education circles, we are beginning to use the term, learning points. We were at a learning point time when we all met here on the porch early into our careers. As young adults, we were searching. We were ready to explore and reshape our identity and future. Granddad spurred our imagination and vision. He turned stories into metaphors that became scenarios in which we could look ahead and see our future, sometimes in parallel journey, sometimes in contrasts. Life has a thousand porches - a thousand learning points, where bigness of spirit can be extended metaphors, where insights become intense defining moments. When I was privileged to be here on this porch with you, it was one big defining moment for me.

Talk about a legacy, Granddad has left us one. And now it's also Grandmother who is extending a legacy, asking us to put our best insights into stories as crossover insights. She has been a school teacher across the years. And that's what I am. It's not just a job, it's a calling. I am not just a teacher. I think of myself as a Big Ten Generation teacher, in residence, on location, like Granddad.

A teacher. That's all I ever wanted to be. Ever since I started kindergarten, I fell in love with teaching. All through school I kept seeing myself standing before a class as a teacher. In college I was an education major and absorbed all the methods and never lost the dream.

Then I found Brian. Or he found me. Either way, I was in love. And out of that, I found my way into a wonderful family of teachers. And, I found Granddad's Big Ten Universal Qualities. It all connected with my calling. I have found a focus for my teaching. I want to tell stories and teach the Big Ten. I want to teach the world to sing, 'we are the world.' I want to help us collaborate - to work together for our best future. And we will never reach that unless we learn how to work together. That's a teacher's calling. And so, that's my word, collaboration.

I think learning how to do that may be the reason Granddad wanted us to meet here on the porch again. Now I will stop. I want to hear your stories."

After a thoughtful moment, Steve said, "bigness of spirit". You used that term and you have already shown us that. And whether you found Brian or he found you, we are fortunate to have your bigness of spirit among us. And we will look forward to how that continues to play out in your story as a teacher. Your students are privileged to have you as their teacher of collaboration. And we are privileged to have you here helping us remember our Granddad in such a special way. Thank you, Linda.

Now, who wants to take another word?" Steve asked.

"I'll do that," Les said. "My teaching is on a college level. But as I listened to Linda talk about teaching children, my mind kept translating that over to an adult level - to a college student level. I began thinking of how the Big Ten qualities could be taught to college students who are deep into shaping an identity for their future and careers, but especially for those who are planning to be teachers of children. It could be a required course in the curriculum. I teach physics, but knowing the Big Ten qualities is far more important than knowing physics. In physics we want to know how the world works. In the Big Ten qualities we want to learn how to make the world work better.

So, my word would be **Integrity**. In science integrity is such a big word. If we are to have integrity with the progression of science, we must make sure what we test in the lab always aligns with how the world works. And if that is a critical expectation in science, should we not have the same expectation for a healthy human identity? Science and faith must be partners. Granddad put the two together.

Many religious people do not do that. They are so caught up in keeping their religion right, they fail to focus on what religion is supposed to be about in the first place - about making humanity right. But let me stop myself and say, 'you didn't ask for a sermon, did you?"

Steve teased. "I thought you were a science teacher. Now you've turned preacher. But it's a pretty good sermon. Keep going."

"Well," Les said, returning the tart. "Preacher or scientist, whichever, the two must never be far apart if we are to build a better future than our past! Science and faith must go hand in hand if we are ever to have integrity.

I teach physics at the university where Granddad was a distinguished professor and philosopher. He modeled what he taught. He knew his philosophy had to align with new information that comes with our age of science and technology. And he knew religion often gets in the way of that by being so caught up in protecting certain theological mythologies that, as a consequence, it pushes newness to one side, missing out on the benefits it could provide if it focused on being a working faith, not just a religion.

Religious people often ignore newness, while they proudly literalize old mythologies as though they were helping God. I know Granddad tried to lead the way beyond that in his classes at the university. He had a faith, not a religion. Everybody on campus respected him for that. That's why his classes are always so full.

It has taken thousands of years to build our progression of knowledge into a faith, and we must have enough integrity to respect the progressive and evolving nature of our journey. And we have such a long way to go yet. So we need integrity with how we see ourselves in the progression of our collective intelligence. I learned a lot about that here on this old porch. Granddad had integrity. He tried to live connected to this higher oneness. Do you know that I am the only one of you who heard Granddad's last sermon at the university? I had no idea it would be his last. He spoke at the University Chapel. At the end of the service, I went up to speak to him while he was shaking hands with faculty and students. 'Great sermon,' I said. 'Is there some way I could get a copy of it?' I asked.

'Oh, yes,' he said in his gracious manner, 'That's easy enough to take care of. Do you mind going to the pulpit and get my iPad and bring it back here and I will just attach it over to your iPhone.'

"Now, I don't know if there is such a thing as an energy field, but when I got to that pulpit, I felt a special kind of energy - an aura of the magnitude of his thinking. It was as though my consciousness was awakened at a new level. Energy field or not, I do know this, our awareness can be lifted by the presence, and by the memory, of people like Granddad."

When Les paused, Steve cut in and said, "Les, let me interrupt a moment. I got to give my memorial tribute while I stood behind the old pulpit where Granddad stood at the beginning of his dreams. And you got to stand in the pulpit at the University Chapel where he gave his last sermon. Please tell me that you saved that sermon in some way."

"Oh, yes," Les said, "I not only kept it, but downloaded it over into my computer to save there, even did a printout. Does that mean that you would like to have a copy?"

"Yes, indeed, but not just for me. I am guessing all of us would like a copy," was Steve's response.

"Consider it done," Les said, "It's like Granddad said to me, 'That's easy enough to take care of.' I have your email addresses and I will send it to you so you can save it in whatever way you choose. As for me, I not only saved it in my documents, but printed it out. It was not only a great sermon, it is treasure I can hold in my hands."

Les turned to Brian and said, "Pardon my philosophizing, but you know me - I like to do that. So, Brian, I would like to hear your take on what I have been saying. Your wife, Linda, is a teacher of children. And you work in a university setting. How do you see it?"

"Much the same as you," Brian responded. "I admit students to the university and I hear them discussing what subjects to choose. It would be good if students had an option to take a course on the Big Ten Universal Qualities. Right now, such a course is not available. But it is so basic to developing a healthy, successful working identity that it needs to be taught. We need a philosophy of life course, Identity 101. As I see it, we all need to have a knowledge-based faith that can be learned for a higher level of living.

So my word would be **Honesty**, especially intellectual honesty. It is important for our ideas to stand up to the scrutiny of the progression of knowledge and be open-ended enough so ideas can to be tested in story. Honesty requires a continuing reach beyond the old so it can be tested by the new. And I just don't see that happening enough. So I keep reaching for openness and honesty."

He paused. "Do I sound like a professor?"

"Yessss!" his cousins joked in concert.

Brian accepted the tease, saying, "Well, I am around professors enough that it may have rubbed off. But I wouldn't mind being one. I just think our professors are among the most honest people I know, and that our Granddad was at the top of that list.

But let me go back to what Linda was saying about our finding each other and being in love. She wasn't sure who found whom. I know which it was. I found her. I wanted to sing out the news.

> I have found her! She's an angel
> With the dust of the stars in her eyes.
> We were dancing, we were flying
> And she's taking me back to the skies.

So, I am the one who did the finding!" As he reached over and took Linda's hand and lifted it up, the cousins began to applaud.

Assuming that was the completion of Brian's story, Steve said, "Let's see now, so far we've used the words, Collaboration, Integrity, and Honesty. Who wants to choose the next one?"

Norman spoke immediately. "I can't top Brian's story, but I'll take one of the words," Norman said. "It's **fairness**. I'm like Linda and Brian, I can almost get up on my stump and make a speech. Are you sure you want to get me started?"

"Not really," Wilson said, continuing the jest of the moment. "But go ahead and we'll decide later."

"It's a big challenge," Norman began, "matching our humanity with the tremendous advances in our technology. **Fairness** is my word. When I see the gap between those who have and those who have not, between societies which have the advantages of science and technology, and societies where so many are left behind, the gap is enormous! That leaves a lot of unfairness. To close that gap will take a long time, and require a tremendous upgrade in our humanity. But, of course, that is not beyond the potential of our time and place in the story. We can work to create some fairness. The gap between what we can do on our own, and what we can do with the help of our newest technology is growing all the time. Life is not fair. It never has been, and may never be. But, we have a chance to do what we can to change the imbalance.

I think Granddad was always trying to change the imbalance by doing what he could to help people find their way to turn challenge into opportunity. Do you remember his saying, 'If we keep trying in the face of our challenges, that is when we find new ways to win. Not before, but while - while we are trying.

I don't know how our grandmother is feeling right now about being left alone, but I haven't heard her crying about how unfair life is. If I know her, she will make a new fairness out of this new phase of her life from this point on. Maybe that's what we have now - a chance to sit on this old porch one more time as an echo of our granddad's stories of new beginnings beyond old endings. And that's likely what Grandmother will be doing - celebrating wonderful yesterdays, but building our best new tomorrows. So, along with Grandmother, that's our opportunity.

I remember those special days we all sat here and heard that positive "can do" approach. You think that hasn't made a difference in my life? It has! We may be far enough down the road now that we are beginning to see even more insights from Granddad's stories than we did then. And what we see is Grandmother, living out the best of human qualities on her new journey. And, of course, we can do that too, where the fairness we keep trying to give to life, is greater than the unfairness that comes from life."

When Norman paused, Mel pitched in, saying, "It's my time now. Wow, Norman, you sound like Granddad. I can almost hear him saying, 'in the worst of times, make sure you are found doing our best of things. He kept talking about being world citizens. He kept saying, 'it's not where we are, but who we are' that gives us our best chance to be world citizens. More and more that's how I see my work with the United Nations - that wherever they ask me to go, there is where I can make my career a major channel of caring. So my word is **caring.**

In connection with my work with the United Nations, I remember that little girl in Kenya. Somewhere in her remote location she had gotten to know a nurse. After that, she was determined that she was going to be a nurse. She didn't have a 'farmhouse porch' but she had a farmhouse porch person in her journey story who modeled how to be caring. It made her want to find her place in the story, as someone who cares, no matter where that would be.

I have followed her story. She is in nursing school now. I don't know where she will serve, but I think I know something about how she will serve. She will be a part of the Big Ten Generation by being one of the caring persons in our new age! I think I know what her word will be in her nursing career. It will be caring. And that's my word. And it's with that frame of mind I will continue my work with the United Nations. Can't you just hear Granddad saying, we don't get to choose all that comes to us in life - just choose what we make of what comes to us. I think I have found a focus for that in the United Nation - in that worldwide symbol of building a better world. And I am proud to be a part of it and want to see how I can make teaching the Big Ten a part of my work in some way. Shouldn't our careers be an expression of our caring? I think so.

So, as I listened to Linda talking about teaching the Big Ten, I could see myself finding some way of teaching the Big Ten as a part of my work with the United Nations in Kenya. It's a part of

Granddad's dream - that the Big Ten be taught in all the learning centers of the world. My confidence is growing. I think I can do that teach these Big Ten Universal Qualities, in some way, on some frontier, for a better world."

The quiet pause which followed Mel's monologue and dream-ahead ideas, seemed to indicate that all of them were respectfully measuring themselves out of a reference to their granddad and the nobility of his legacy as an identity to live up to.

"Well," Steve said, "I can see getting this group started is not a problem. And that's good. The intensity of this time together may never come again but what a privilege these moments have been. We can continue them, but right now we may need to take a break. So let's take a fifteen minute break and come right back and continue these reflections that are becoming scenarios for our place in the story."

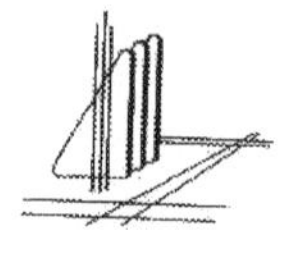

Chapter Three

Legacy

"He was an artist in telling stories."

As they all gathered back on the porch, after the break, Steve said, "We all know from our session so far, that Granddad and Grandmother's grandchildren are not short on ideas. So let's go again. Who wants to tell a story next?"

"I will," Wilson said. "I'm a cousin in this group by my marriage to Marsha. Even so, I want to get into the lineup to express my admiration for Granddad. He was a person of great tolerance. So, my word is **Tolerance.**

I want to go back to my understanding of Granddad's major thesis - the great divide between transcendence and immanence - between authority and openness. We have been the human family on earth for thousands of years, and during that time we have had many religions based in authority, which have so often been short on tolerance. The transcendence paradigm of a God, out there, who has already set destiny, is the major paradigm that has swept down through the centuries in many mythologies, religions, and recurring traditions. Hasn't worked very well. Hasn't made the world family tolerant. Divided us into 'us' and 'them,' even fighting each other, and starting new religions. The pressing need of our time is not to win a contest about who's right and who's wrong, but to have the kind of tolerance that overarches and goes beyond our differences. We have made progress in science and technology, but what about our humanity, as Granddad asked? Can we live under an umbrella large enough to find a new level of oneness beyond our differences? Can we, or will we, move beyond whatever duplicates history's ancient 'sticks and stones' conflicts, enough to define our oneness on our little planet as part of the expansive oneness of what may be an endless universe? For this we need tolerance. To me, Granddad was a model of tolerance. I felt that when I was privileged to join this family.

When I married Marsha, and when Linda married Brian, Granddad just adopted us as his newest grandchildren, and we adopted him as our special Granddad! What a privilege to be sitting here on Granddad's farmhouse porch, sharing with cousins who are extending Granddad's legacy of tolerance."

When Wilson paused, Marsha said, "My time now. I am so pleased to hear my husband speak so respectfully of this family. A word closely related to tolerance is respect. That's my word, **respect**. Granddad respected all of us, and we respected him and Grandmother.

I am beginning to get the picture, pun intended. As an artist, pictures are my world. But what is so special about this old porch is that it's here that Granddad painted those word-pictures that define our best tomorrows. His word-pictures live on in my mind. As I listen to you, I know they live on in your minds, too. Gathering here on the porch again is a wonderful place to recognize that Granddad was an artist with words and stories. He wove them into a defining framework for a wholesome and healthy identity for our time in history.

Let me tell you about my own personal porch time with

Granddad. I was here with my parents one day, and Granddad and I were out here on the porch, talking about metaphors. I asked him if heaven was just a metaphor. And he said, 'That's what it is. It's an ideal. It's a reach for the ultimate of goodness. Trouble is, all too often people have made it a place, far, far away. Out of reach. Up there. Beyond. But that's not what Jesus emphasized. The central metaphor of Jesus was a kingdom of heaven we can live out in our story now, on earth, not one we have to die before we reach it. Milton was closer to that perspective than many people when he said, 'the mind is it's own place.'

Granddad said, 'In terms of painting, many artists have tried to depict heaven as up there, and from where angels are always coming down here. But our best understanding, heaven is that it is an ideal we reach for and get as close to as we can down here. It's a reach for the good, a reach for what's better, a level of goodness we put into life by the way we care about our fellowman. It's not vertical. It's horizontal. It's not transcendence. It's immanence. It's not religious. It's humanitarian. It's not easy to put on canvas, but I want you to paint that perspective as best you can. Perhaps Albrecht Durer got close to that when he painted Praying Hands, showing respect for the sacrifice his brother had made for him by working in the mines so he could learn to paint.'

I was listening intently when Granddad said, 'Marsha, try to find and paint your version of praying hands. Try to find ways to show the contrast between selfishness and generosity. Show respect for the mystery of oneness - create parallels to the mystery of how water stays water because the elements work together. Paint the oneness of goodwill and kindness. Do what you can to paint the Big Ten Universal Qualities. Paint your version of the poem by Sam Walter Foss, 'The House by the Side of the Road.'

> It's here the race of men go by,
> They are good, they are bad, they are weak, they
> are strong,

Wise, foolish - so am I;
Then why should I sit in the scorner's seat,
Or hurl the cynic's ban?
Let me live in my house by the side of the road
And be a friend to man.[1]

Don't paint yesterday; paint tomorrow,' he said. 'Paint what is important in our human story as a vision of our best. Find your ways to paint courage and honor, tolerance and understanding. Paint what's wholesome and uplifting. Paint caring and kindness, honesty and respect, you know, all the best qualities that can be lived out down on the dusty roads of life, like Jesus modeled when he washed his disciples' feet. Instead of painting a grandiose distant heaven, paint the qualities of our best humanity down here on earth. Paint those qualities that make us world citizens.'

In all my art training, I have never had an art teacher get any closer to defining great art than Granddad did that day. It's all fresh as yesterday, now that we are sitting here on this old porch again. It's a kind of epiphany. I want to paint life's farmhouse porch visions.

Being here again makes me want to go to my studio and paint my best picture ever of humanity's best tomorrow. I know I can't ignore humanity's worst, but I want to go beyond that to paint a new picture of humanity's best, where a better tomorrow is like a new sunrise on the horizon. How I wish I could put that kind of hope on canvas. And I will. It may not be immediate, but Granddad's respect for the oneness of all existence and the sunrise of a new oneness for humanity will find its way into my paintings. You, and the ideas you are sharing here will be a part of that kind of imagination out of which I will paint, not only who we are, but who we can become.

Steve, in your memorial tribute to Granddad, you quoted James

[1] Sam Walter Foss. "House by the Side of the Road"

Weldon Johnson's poem and song. We sing that song in our church services and I want to keep singing it until it flows over into my paintings and my story.

Sing a song full of the faith that the dark past has taught us;
Sing a song full of the hope that the present has brought us;
Facing the rising sun of our new day begun,
Let us march on till victory is won.

I want to paint 'the rising sun of our new day begun.' Granddad did that in his word pictures. As a tribute of respect, I want to paint new tomorrows on canvas. If I can do that it will extend the legacy of our very special Granddad."

Silence followed. It was a silence of respect and admiration for the way Marsha had captured a word picture of Granddad. Then Steve said, "Marsha, you could have been the one standing behind that old pulpit instead of me."

"That's it," Marsha said, as a burst of insight. "That's one picture I will paint - that old pulpit, with dreamers standing there, painting new dreams."

Steve paused a long moment, then said, "Thank you, Marsha. I had tears in my eyes when I stood behind that old pulpit. Now it's about to happen again. Paint that picture for all of us!"

Steve was reflecting as he said, "What I need to be sure of now is that all ten of the Big Ten qualities are being included. As best I can determine, there are three of us who haven't told a story yet. Three words are left, diplomacy, nobility, and kindness. Who want to choose? Then I will choose the remaining word."

Sue did not hesitate. "Kindness is the word I would like to have, and if I may, I would like to be last,"

Steve turned to Sandra and said, "Which of the two is your choice?"

"**Nobility** is the word I would like to talk about," Sandra said. "That way you can be the diplomat and choose diplomacy."

Steve responded in a jovial manner. "Then when it's my time I will choose diplomacy. Sandra, would you like to begin?"

Sandra began by saying very sincerely, "I am pleased to have the privilege of being one of the Kelly grandchildren. Like Wilson and Brian, I am one of Granddad and Grandmother's three adopted grandchildren. As I have been listening to all of you, I realize what a high privilege that is. I am the only one who wasn't here for your earlier meeting here on the porch when Granddad told his stories. But I have had the privilege of being here on this porch. That was when Steve and I were planning our wedding ceremony and we came here and sat on this old porch with Grandmother and Granddad and planned it so that Granddad's favorite words of the Big Ten were a part of our commitment to each other.

When I was in seminary I read the books by Dr. James Kelly. Those books reset my thinking. They were not about theology. They were about life.

Then, as by a special coincidence, or whatever you want to call it, I met Dr. Kelly's grandson, Steve. He showed up at the World Citizen Church where I was serving as minister. That led to our meeting on the deck of Dr. David Logan's retreat house on the peaks of Eagles View Mountain. We met there more than once and made a discovery. We were in love. And standing there by the handrail, Steve asked me to marry him. And I said, 'I'll think about it.' No, no, I am just joking, big time. I said, 'YES.'

That led to that first time I sat on this old porch where we planned our wedding ceremony and made the words of the Big Ten Universal Qualities a part of the commitment we made to each other. One of those words is nobility. What I realize so much now is that I married into nobility. And that's not flattery. That's for real. Nobility is what you have been talking about here as each of you told your stories about Granddad as your personal memorial tribute.

Nobility has to do with obligation and responsibility by reason of rank or birth. *Noblesse oblige.* Nobility obligates. High privilege leads to and new opportunity and responsibility. All of us are highly privileged to be a part of the legacy of Dr. James Kelly. Granddad."

Breaking a moment of silence and reflection that followed Sandra's respectful tribute, Steve said, "My word is **diplomacy**. Diplomacy is making things fit together so they achieve good solutions. The influence of Granddad's life, his stories, and his books have opened a new understanding of how un-chosen pathways can become opportunity pathways. His writings unveil new insights like a series of surprises. I was in my PhD program when I had a chance to live in Alpine on the peaks of Eagles View Mountain. The first Sunday after I began living there, I came down that twisting road to attend a service at what was once known as Grovemont Church. By the time I visited that first Sunday, the name had been changed to World Citizen Church. It was on that Sunday morning that I met Sandra Millan. And you just heard how that turned out.

Along with getting to know Sandra, I met Dr. David Logan, who for several years had been inviting students to live in his retreat cabin, on Eagles View, for the summer while they worked on special studies. Not long after that, the three of us met and sat on the deck overlooking Alpine, and began to dream. Out of those dreams the World Citizen Center came into being.

Granddad came to the grand opening, and appropriately so. His lectures and books were vital to the vision out of which it began. The center is focused on the Big Ten Universal Qualities and how they can be adopted as a healthy identity for anyone, anytime, and anywhere in the human family as an overarching framework for world citizenship. The more you know about the World Citizen

Center, the more you know it was inspired by the writings of Granddad.

Diplomacy has to do with creating worthy goals as common objectives and vision and then working together to achieve those objectives. Somebody has to see a picture, not only of what is, but of what ought to be and lead the way to that. Granddad did that.

So, here we are on the old porch of dreams. It's time to dream anew. It's time to think out best thoughts, to turn old endings into new beginnings, to give our best dreams their best chance to happen. Yesterday must not be allowed to hold back tomorrow. Does that sound like Granddad? We all heard it here on this porch. It's here we could dream and see sunrise tomorrows.

After a pause, Steve said, "Sue, there's one of the Big Ten words left. You get to choose that."

Sue began respectfully. "Like I chose earlier, my word is **Kindness**. It leads all the others. You remember Granddad called it the magic word in the homecoming talk he made at New Home Church that Sunday at the end of our porch seminar. It's an overarching word. It's the word that makes the sun come up as a smile on the face. It's the word that comes to mind when we think of our grandparents. In fact, this farmhouse could well have a smiley face on its front door. Kindness is inside. It's outside. Here on the porch. It's down in the meadow. Kindness lived here. Now it's in our memory banks in a special way.

Do you remember the charge Granddad gave to me that summer we were all gathered here? He knew I was the one who loved this place so much. He said, 'Now, Sue, you must never sell this place. Keep it as a gathering place for the whole family, for children and children's children. Make it a place where you learn from nature. Make it a place where you catch some glimpse of the oneness of all existence. Make it a place of dreams.' It was his Walden Pond. It has become our Farmhouse Porch Walden Pond. No wonder he wanted us to meet here again after his memorial service. So, it's not just a place, it's a framework for identity. It's a legacy we have now inherited."

Silence fell on the porch. No one said anything for the next minute. Aware that this was an ending, waiting for a new beginning, Steve stood up and the others followed his unspoken lead and began to give each other handshakes and hugs. One by one, they drifted quietly back into the farmhouse to connect with family and friends who had gathered in honor and memory of the beloved and respected, Dr. James Kelly.

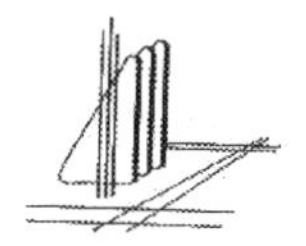

Chapter Four

Dear Cousins,

When we all sat on the farmhouse porch following Granddad's memorial service, I indicated that I had a digital copy of his last sermon. Upon Steve's request, I am sending it to you. You may choose to do as I have done, make your own hard copy of it and keep it as a treasured statement of Granddad's positive faith. So, here is Dr. James Kelly's last sermon.

Les

Shaping Our Best Future

By James Kelly

"As I stand at this pulpit of our University Chapel, I can't help but think, this grand pulpit has been the place where scholars and leading speakers have spoken across decades. I am humbly privileged to stand here as part of that succession. As a professor here, I have sat many times where you now sit, listening with respect as speakers have spoken from this privileged place. Now I have the privilege of speaking to you as a new generation who continue the search for understanding, insight, and hope for tomorrow. It is no small moment for me as I seek to honor this platform of responsibility for our place in the story.

My iPad is in place here on the pulpit with my message on it, but I really won't need to follow it as I openly share understandings out of my journey of life. The title of my message is four words, 'Shaping Our Best Future.'

I want to invite you to think along with me. In fact, I am asking you to do more than think, I am asking you to dream about tomorrow with great respect for where we have arrived in our time in history, and are now taking our place in the moving human story. We have a place in the story. But we also have an opportunity to shape that story. We can shape that story in the perspective of Charles Dickens, who said, 'it was the best of times; it was the worst of times.' We have a unique opportunity to dream our best dreams, and do what we can to make this the best of times.

Stories are metaphors that reach across the centuries. Four writers told a story about a person who stood at a crossroads in history and looked with respect on yesterday, but who looked ahead with even greater respect on tomorrow. These writers told the story of one of the great thinkers of all time who dreamed a new paradigm for how we can define the times as the best of times – to build a kingdom of heaven on earth.

Luke was the writer who saw the magnitude of this man's story, not only in terms of where he was born, or the time times in which he lived, but as a model a great life. He told the story of Jesus of Nazareth as though his story was a part of the mysterious wonders of all existence. Out of his respect and high esteem for this world citizen, he wrote,

> *There were in the same country shepherds abiding in the field, keeping watch over their flock by night. And, lo, the*

> *angel of the Lord came upon them, and the glory of the Lord shone round about them: and they were sore afraid. And the angel said unto them, Fear not: for, behold, I bring you good tidings of great joy, which shall be to all people. For unto you is born to you in the city of David a Saviour, which is Christ the Lord. And this shall be a sign unto you; Ye shall find the babe wrapped in swaddling clothes, lying in a manger.*
>
> *And suddenly there was with the angel a multitude of the heavenly hosts praising God, and saying, Glory to God in the highest, and on earth peace, goodwill toward men.* Luke 2: 8-14 KJV

We recognize this as the spectacular announcement of the birth of Jesus. It's a story that was told out of awe and admiration. If you ask questions about the nature of the angels that appeared, you spoil the story. If you try to tweak it so it fits with today's understanding of science, you distract from the mythology out of which the storyteller told the story. It's a story that announces the beginning of a wonderful life, set in the context of those times. But that story is also about a person who sought to shape a better tomorrow than yesterday.

The story teller began his story with the birth of a baby, laid in a manger and given the name of Jesus. It only briefly tells about when he was growing up as a boy, and when he went to school, like any of the other boys in Nazareth, and when they read the proverbs of Solomon. When those admiring writers told his story, they told about a man who became a great Teacher, who dreamed of a new tomorrow - a kingdom of heaven on earth. People were ready to listen to that Teacher and followed him wherever he went. He enlisted some disciples to be his students and they respected him as the Master Teacher. Not only did his disciples follow him day after day to learn from him, but people by the hundreds gathered in as close as they could and listened with great interest.

On one of those days long ago, a little boy was among those who came to listen. He stood on the hillside and looked out over one of those crowds who had come to hear this Teacher. That little boy stood there wishing he could be up close enough so he could see better and hear the Teacher.

Earlier that day, just as the sun was coming up over the little home where he lived, he was excited because his mother was going to let him go all by himself to hear the great teacher. His mother fixed him a lunch of two biscuits and five little fish and folded them neatly in a napkin and put them in a little basket for him to take.

"Son," she said, "I hope you have a good day and get to hear Jesus. And when you get back home this evening, I want you to tell me all about it."

"Oh, I will, mother. I will," he said quickly." He thanked his mother for the little lunch, reached up and kissed her and skipped out the door and down the path to the road on his way to hear Jesus.

When he got to where Jesus was speaking, there were lots and lots of people. There were so many people that he couldn't even see Jesus. Wishing he could get up closer, he began to nudge his way through the crowd, the way little boys can, until he got up close enough to see Jesus. That's when he realized he was right up there among the disciples. One of them said, "Hi, Sonny, Do you see Jesus?"

"Oh, yes," he answered.

Then the disciple said, "Oh, I see you brought your lunch with you."

"Yes" the little boy said. "I have two pieces of bread and five little fish. But Jesus has been talking about how hungry everybody is going to be before they get back home. Jesus may get hungry too. I am not very hungry and I wish Jesus could have my lunch. Would you give it to him for me?"

"I will if that's what you really want," the disciple said.

"Here," the little boy said, as he pushed his basket lunch into the hands of the disciple. "At least Jesus can have something to eat."

"My name is James," the disciple said as he reached out and took the little boy's lunch, much to the surprise of his brother, John, whose expression seemed to say, "What? You are going to take that little boy's lunch?"

James didn't say anything, just took the little boys lunch to Jesus and said, 'Jesus, there is a little boy here who has a little lunch and he wants you to have it.'

Jesus looked over at the little boy and smiled as he took the little basket. He held it in hands as he looked up to heaven and thanked God for the little boys and girls, and for the little lunch this little boy had shared. And that's when a miracle happened.

There are great stories we cannot live without if we want to define how Jesus represented the highest qualities people can choose to live by. This is one of those stories. When we update that little boy's story to our time it becomes a basket of insight for how we can share our best qualities in the greatest age the world family has ever known.

And do we ever have an opportunity to dream new tomorrows when we consider the progression up to our time when grocery stores provide our bread and fish! Our basket is full! What a story we have to tell about the growing potential of our science and technology to multiply our human potential to shape our best future!

That evening when that little boy ran up the path to his house, he had a story he just couldn't wait to tell. He bounced in the door with excitement, and began calling, "Mother. Mother. Oh, Mother, you know that little lunch you gave me this morning - you know what I did with it?"

"No, son," she said as she looked into his beaming face. "What did you do with it? It was enough, wasn't it?" she asked.

"Oh, yes. It was enough. More than enough. But I didn't eat

it. I gave it to Jesus. You know those men who always follow Jesus around, his disciples, I gave it to one of them. James, he's the one. I told him that I wasn't very hungry and that I wanted Jesus to have that lunch you fixed for me. So he took my lunch and gave it to Jesus. And Jesus took it and looked over at me with the biggest and bestest smile I have ever seen. He held my little lunch in his hands and looked up into heaven and began to thank God for little boys and girls, and for that little lunch I had given to him.

Then I saw Jesus go over to a young family with my lunch in his hands. There were four children there. Jesus told their mother about my lunch I had given to him. He said, "I am sure the little boy who gave it to me would be glad if I shared some of it with your children."

But that's when the mother said, 'I brought some lunch too. Maybe we could put it together with ours and ask that little boy to join us.' So mother, I went over and joined them and became a part of their picnic right there. I don't think anyone went away hungry. There was enough for everybody. In fact, those twelve men who follow Jesus, disciples, that's what they call themselves, all of them went around and gathered what was left over. It was the biggest picnic I have ever seen! Oh, Mother, do you think it was one of his miracles?"

She looked into his face and said, "Yes, son. I think it was. I think it was one of his miracles."

That's a story we cannot live without in our time if we want to recreate miracles in our time. It's the story of the Teacher, born in Bethlehem, who defined and modeled sharing and multiplying our resources.

What about miracles in our time? I am not talking about the miracle of your getting an A on that last test when you know you studied only enough to make a C. That's just wishing.

Are there real miracles we can believe in for our time? I think so! Wonderful miracles we all can believe in. When we do experiments in our laboratories which show the marvelous dependability of all existence for billions of years, that's a miracle we can believe in. When we learn more about the ways the world works so we can work with it in fantastic new ways, that's a miracle we can believe in. When we use the progression of knowledge and its tools of technology to help us be build the larger common good for the human family, that's a miracle we can believe in. When we learn to do unto others as we would have them do unto us, that's a miracle we can believe in. And when we link our science and technology with the Big Ten Universal Qualities, that a miracle we can believe in and make happen. That miracle is up to us. We are its designers and creators.

Some of you students here today are trying to learn how to work with the way the world works in your physics classes. Some of you are choosing engineering as your way of designing the products we need for our growing world family. Some of you are in the social sciences where you want to help the human family share compassion and caring across all boundaries until we see our tomorrows in terms of the oneness of the human family. We all have a basket - doctors, nurses, farmers, retailers, manufactures, all of us - all of us have a basket out of which we can share.

And teachers and education majors, I haven't forgotten about your place in the story. Oh, no! Your basket is large and one of the most important baskets. Your basket can be carried to all the learning centers of the world. All your colleagues need you and what is in your basket! The need is to have thousands and thousands, millions, of learning centers where the big dream of a partnership of our sciences and important technologies are aligned with, and by, the identity framework of the Big Ten Universal Qualities. That's the miracle boys and girls in our time need to be able tell mothers and fathers about, as their dreams for sunrise tomorrows.

Building our talents and skills into careers that make a better world, that's the miracle that can happen here on the university campus. Increasing our value and defining who we are as people of: kindness, caring, honesty, respect, collaboration, tolerance, fairness, integrity, diplomacy, and nobility, those identity words are in our basket to share. Making those choices which multiply the wonders of our information-digital-molecular age into the greatest age the world has ever known, that's in our basket. All this potential for achieving a higher quality of life for a better world - that is the exciting story that little boys and girls can't wait to tell!

So, that little boy looked up at his mother and asked, 'Oh, Mother, do you think it was one of his miracles?"

His mother looked down at his beaming face and said, "I think it was, son. I think it was."

That's a story we can't live without. And that kind of miracle of sharing our resources of knowledge and power for the larger good is one we need to try to make real in our story.

When the storyteller of long ago told about a baby who became that Master Teacher, and who took a little boy's lunch one day and shared it, that storyteller just couldn't wait to tell his story in terms of the wonders of all existence, and a model for how to live by a dream of sharing as a world family.

So, when he told his story about the Master Teacher who was born in Bethlehem, he said,

> *And suddenly there was with the angel a multitude of the heavenly hosts praising God, and saying, Glory to God in the highest, and on earth peace, goodwill toward men.*
>
> *And it came to pass, as the angels were gone away from them into heaven, the shepherds said one to another, Let us now go even unto Bethlehem, and see this thing which has come to pass." Luke 2:15 KJV*

Two words are at the summit of our place in the story in our greatest age of unparalleled potential for new tomorrows - *noblesse oblige.* Nobility obligates.

Three questions become questions for all of us now that we have been born into the marvel of our digital-information-molecular age. To what nobility were we born? What are we going to do with it?" What's in our basket?

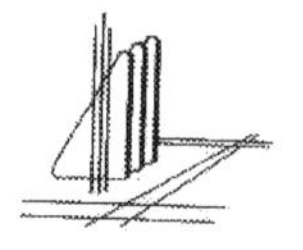

Chapter Five

A New Place In Dreams

"No boy or girl anywhere should ever have to say,
"I never was taught the Big Ten Universal Qualities!"

THE SEASONS WERE BLENDING INTO ANOTHER SPRINGTIME IN ALPINE. The mountain slopes were being painted with sweeping strokes of light green and delicate touches of soft pink, created by new leaves and the first blossoms of redbud and maple trees. Eagles View Mountain was a place of dreams.

Following the Sunday morning worship service at World Citizen Church, Dr. David Logan was among those shaking hands with Dr. Sandra, saying very sincerely, "Dr. Sandra, the service was extraordinary. Maybe we could reflect on it further if we met for lunch up on Eagles View. Steve and I have been in touch by phone and have set up tentative plans for the three of us to have lunch together up there. We were quite aware that we might have to adjust the time in order to fit with your schedule. So, are you free for lunch today?"

"Oh yes, I'm free, especially since we would be meeting at your place up on Eagles View." Sandra replied immediately. "I look forward to being up there. I already know that Steve has something he wants to share with you. So, yes, I am free for lunch together."

"Great! Here's the plan." Dr. Logan said. "I will go by the Crestline Restaurant and order a take-out meal for all of us. By that time, you are likely to be free. Then you and Steve can come up to my cabin and we can have lunch on the deck. And, oh, bring a sweater, or coat. It's still early springtime up there. But if it is too cool, we will go inside and sit by the fireplace. Does that work for you?"

"Yes, indeed," Sandra responded enthusiastically. "Steve and I would welcome that very much. Eagles View is a very special place for both of us."

"Then I'll meet you there," Dr. Logan said, as he moved on to let others shake hands with their much admired and respected minister.

Eagles View was a place they all felt at home. Setting out their lunch on the table there on the deck was an easy flow of simple and basic preparations.

"Dr. Logan," Steve said, as he leaned against the deck banister, "you get the credit for this being a very special place in the story for Sandra and me. Standing here by this handrail is where Sandra and I were engaged, You get the credit for that. It never would have happened without the very unique opportunity you gave me to study up here that summer. Now, what a privilege to be up here again and look down on World Citizen Church and on the magnificent World Citizen Center, where so much has come together in such a short time."

"Well," Dr. Logan said with a smile of recognition, "I have never been accused of being matchmaker before. In this case, I will accept the title and assure you it was totally unplanned, but I am pleased to have been a part of it in some way. You two belong together."

As they opened their box lunches and began eating, Dr. Logan launched into a story about a church he had attended the previous

Sunday, where a prayer of confession was part of the service. "Sandra, I know we have talked about this before. In fact, it was the center of what we talked about that first time we met in your office. But, that kind of addiction to yesterday's paradigms was a part of a church service I attended this past Sunday. It still bugs me!

The Prayer of Confession was almost painful. I never saw anything so out of touch with where we are in our time, when we need to be looking forward at our potential instead of looking back at our failures, then apologizing to God for them. Prayers like that are like making our failures a hallmark of self-depreciation, and a putdown that God is not at all likely to be interested in hearing from the prize of all creation, the human family. Speaking very anthropomorphically, I bet God gets mighty tired of hearing that kind of thing. And, if I get the drift of one paradigm about God, it is that he already knows everything about us anyway, and doesn't need a constant reminder of our failed yesterdays.

What God probably would like to hear, would be about a creative, bold, dream we have for the future, not just an empty reconstruction of the past. So I just sat there until they got through apologizing to God, bemoaning their failures, and begging his forgiveness, instead of celebrating their successes. Next Sunday they are likely to repeat the same narrative of negatives, and apologize again for the same sins. It's enough to make God turn his cell phone off. And, it makes me want never to go to that kind of church again.

So, Dr. Sandra, you just don't know how refreshing it was to be a participant in the service you led today. The affirmation of faith you used was in considerable contrast to the one last Sunday. The one for today was an announcement of new beginnings. Your people have learned it by memory, so I figured I should, also. Let's see how I can do with it.

I will face this day with faith, hope, and love.
I will draw afresh upon those uplifting forces.

I will be generous in friendship.
I will energize myself with the kindness I give to others.
I will seek to be successful in the great ventures of life.
I will seek to increase my value as a person by
my service to others.
I will continue to picture myself as I want to be
and announce myself to that goal again and again.

Sandra responded with enthusiasm. "That's pretty good. In fact, it's great."

"Well, it kind of flows, so it's easy to memorize. Now, if we can bridge that kind of positive and visionary reach for the future over into the World Citizen Center, it will help people live out those rewarding dynamics of faith in their own identity story right here in Alpine. No one needs to travel anywhere else in the world in order to be a world citizen, just live out world citizen qualities on location here in Alpine.

But I am wondering if you have any new ideas we need to talk about."

"Well, yes," Sandra said, "but not so much mine, as Steve's. I think he's ready to explore a new venture with you."

Steve had been listening while he was leaning on the handrail of the deck, looking out across the valleys below. He turned to Dr. Logan. "Yes," he said reflectively, "I do have a new idea I've been waiting to share with you at the right time and place.

Let me put some pieces of a puzzle together. This is a great place up here that you share so generously. I can see how any student would welcome the chance to spend a summer up here. What I marvel at is that I got to share it. It was like a dream when I got the invitation to come up here to study. So, thank you so much, Dr. Logan. Your sharing it with me opened up a series of new places in a dream.

The first Sunday I was here, I drove down to Alpine and, as a very special coincidence, I met Sandra at her church and we quickly became very close friends. Then soon, more than close friends. Some time after that we were up here on this deck when Sandra and I became engaged. And up here is where the dream for the World Citizen Center began.

Now this is where I would like to explore another piece of that dream that goes beyond the World Citizen Center being only a place for great speakers to share the platform to roll out their studies, research findings, and courageous new ideas. That phase has been a real success! But I keep asking myself if we are underutilizing this magnificent place. Perhaps there is a new phase we should consider that in no way diminishes or interferes with the great speakers platform phase. Allow me to preface that idea.

When I was in college, I worked with a program called Teens Second Chance. I used Granddad's novel, *Apple Blossom Time,* as a story base to help young people find their way beyond big disappointments and failures to a new beginning. Some of those young people have never gotten out of my mind. Here in Alpine, I see their counterpart - young people who need to know about The Big Ten Universal Qualities, and find their own new tomorrows, the way Ru did in the *Apple Blossom Time* novel.

So, here's the new dream. In a nutshell. We would like to start a program in which the Big Ten qualities are taught here at the World Citizen Center, and out of that, to be taught in the Sunday School classes of many churches, in schools, clubs, homes, and in a variety of other learning centers.

But I have an idea about a program that could precede that. Sandra and I have talked about this and we are very excited about the idea. We want to have a series of Parenting Conferences that help parents make their home into one of the learning centers that Dr. Kelly talked about so many times. Recently it dawned on me like an epiphany. The home! That's the key learning center in Dr. Kelly's dream.

I remember hearing Dr. Kelly say, in Martin Luther oratorical style, 'I have a dream that the Big Ten Universal Qualities can be incorporated into all the world family's learning centers and identity paradigms! I have a dream that these qualities can be taught and learned as a framework for a healthy, rewards-based identity which, when embraced by any person, anywhere, anytime, on location that will lead to a successful life and greater future!' I heard him say, "No boy or girl anywhere should ever have to say, I never was taught the Big Ten Universal Qualities!" But near his final days, I heard him say, 'I know I will never live to see the teaching part of my dream completed. That's why it is important to launch a new Big Ten Generation as carriers of this dream.' That's when it occurred to me, the home, that's it, that is the key learning place. Parents are the teachers of the Big Ten Universal Qualities in Dr. Kelly's dream! Inspire the parents of the world so they will teach the Big Ten! The way we can begin, is to have a series of conferences on, Parenting As A Partnership With Children.

But I offer the idea with a considerable caution. The caution comes at the point where we can talk about it, but we don't have the financial resources to do anything about that kind of new program for the center. And we don't know the extent to which you want to keep financing an expansion of the World Citizen Center. What we are dreaming costs money.

I keep thinking of a story about a preacher who was talking to his congregation about a new program he wanted to launch. He was heralding his dream with enthusiasm from the pulpit when he said, 'We have some of this program already in place, but it is just in the walking stage. But we want to take it beyond walking stage, up to the running stage.'

And the brothers and sisters said, 'A-men. Let her run!'

Then the preacher said, 'If this program is going to get past walking stage and the running stage, we need to get it up to the flying stage.'

And the brothers and sisters said, 'A-men. Let her fly.'

Then the preacher said, 'If this program is going to get past walking and past running up to flying, it's going to cost money.'

That's when the A-mens stopped and they said, 'Let her walk, brother. Let her walk.'

After they all laughed at the story, Steve said, "So, what we are talking about is like flying, it's going to cost money. And we don't know if the Vision Foundation will be ready to say, 'Let her walk,' or 'A-men. Let her fly!'

Steve waited for some kind of sign from Dr. Logan. He leaned back against the banister and waited.

"I understand your reluctance," Dr. Logan said, "but there should no reluctance. Dream ahead. Let her fly. We started with a dream. Why stop now? We must always have a dream that keeps leading us. It's like that phrase in South Pacific, 'if you don't have a dream, how you gonna have a dream come true.'

Let me tell you where I am with the Vision Foundation. When someone inherits a base of financial resources, like I did, and when that base expands as the years pass, one gets to the point of saying, 'what can I do with the obligation that accumulating capital resources create?' Just putting it into a foundation and letting it sit there, that's not a good answer. So, I keep looking for some great causes that need to be funded. It's more than venture capital. It's investment in a venture idea, in a dream, in a cause whose time has come in our time in history. So let me say that I respect your caution, but at the same time, I need you to know that when we began the World Citizen Center, I was looking for a great cause worthy of accumulating resources. I was in search of some worthy pioneering venture that needed to happen in our time in history. And I found it! I mean, we found it. And I still marvel at what has happened and the wonderful privilege it has been for me to be a part of that dream. Neither I, or the Foundation, are at an end of that kind of search.

So your idea may be the beginning of a new phase. Feel free to tell me what you are talking about that can help expand that last word of the Big Ten qualities - that summit word that is about the obligation that goes with privilege. You know, *noblesse oblige*. Privilege involves responsibility. We all inherit a cadre of privileges out of which we can do something good if we align resources with important causes. So I like your idea about a new phase. Follow the dream. It may be a part of your catching the torch that your Granddad passed on to you. With great confidence in the two of you to lead the dream, I am ready to say, 'Amen. Let her fly!'

Dr. Logan stood, walked over and put his hands on the handrail as he looked across the valley. When he turned back around, he paused, then said, "Steve, our dreams up here have already opened up dreams for me beyond anything I ever imagined when I began letting students come up here in the summertime to work on their dissertations. I can hardly believe what has happened! And I am listening with great interest. Knowing where we are as the World Citizen Center, is such an excellent beginning. But now we may be at another beginning point.

After a deliberate pause, Dr. Logan said, "Steve, catching that torch may include your doing something else, something you need to make sure is a part of your story. It has to do with something your granddad would want to be a part of his legacy.

Let me explain. You came here to write your dissertation. But it has been detoured by your helping to create the World Citizen Center. And for that I am deeply grateful. We could never have done it without your leadership. Now, the way I see it, you need to let that sit on the sideline enough for you to bring your dissertation front and center. You need your doctoral degree as a platform from which you can explore future options. Your leadership will hit a kind of ceiling unless you also become, Doctor Steve Kelly.

You need that degree to fulfill the stewardship of the potential of your mind and your leadership role as a new visionary in our time. You need it to enlarge your service. You need to keep the detour from becoming a destination. You need it to take up the torch your granddad wanted to pass along to you as a new, Dr. Kelly.

Out of my career as a professor, and in association with leaders of the future, I see that. But, of course, an idea like this is no good unless you see it, and it is also your idea. Can you buy into this as part of your identity and your future at this point?"

Steve answered with a sense of affirmation. "I can. Coming from you, it's like advice coming from Granddad. I respect that. I came here to write my dissertation and I have never considered not finishing it. I am ready for this new focus. Thank you, Dr. Logan, but how does it all fit together now?"

Dr. Logan spoke immediately and said, "Now let me add to what I have suggested. Even though you have moved down to the parsonage, I want to expand your access to this place of vision up here on Eagles View. It's a great place to build important perspectives. I want to offer my cabin as a place to work on your dissertation. Take as long as you need. I am not here that much, and when I want to be here, I can just check in at the delightful bed and breakfast inn near the church. I like staying there and being pampered the way they do.

But, now, one more thing, and it's for you, Sandra. Can you buy into this? Many doctoral candidates never complete their dissertation. They neglect to put in the kind of intentional work it takes, or they get sidetracked by some other phase of life. So, Sandra, an idea like this needs your support, even your sacrifice for him to have the time and space to work on it seriously. Does this kind of quest have your support?"

"Indeed it does," Sandra replied without hesitation. "It's something I want for Steve. But as I look at what Steve has helped to make real, the World Citizen Center, it may not have really been a detour at all, but an important backdrop for his dissertation."

Steve responded with thanks to both Sandra and Dr. Logan, as if to say, 'got it.' "Actually, I am not too far from completing it," Steve said, then launched back into his new idea for the World Citizen Center.

"The new phase will begin with a Parenting Conference which will have some of the characteristics of a big motivation rally. I am very excited about it. It's in line with my dreams. It's like what Robert Frost said, 'way leads on to way.' What you are calling a detour may be a part of my objectives. It's like what they say, one can never write deeply until one has lived deeply. I see this new program as a way to live deeply.

Believing in possibilities is what we are about anyway. When the Wright brothers went to Kitty Hawk to try out their flying machine, perhaps there were some people who thought - crazy guys, they think they can fly. And, likewise, while we are trying to make the Big Ten come alive through this parenting program, there may be some people who think we are out of our minds. But leaders have to walk upfront. I dare to believe that, unique to the place we have in the story here in Alpine, we can actually reshape the future by getting parents to intentionally teach the Big Ten to their children!

The new Parenting Conference will be a kind of test. Each of the speakers we enlist will have the same directive. They will be asked to tell a story, or narrate in essays, about how to be a great parent while making the Big Ten Universal Qualities the identity markers they live by and test in their own experience. I will ask them to dare to speak out of their related professions, and to be brassy enough to talk about their own journey. I want them to springboard out of real time journey stories and experiences, studies, and research to advance the dream of being Big Ten citizens.

I know, that's laying it on pretty heavy, but I don't want to end up with just another college lecture to parents. I want down to earth, practical application, tested in the crucible of real life. What I really want is a Big Ten motivation event that stretches across three great parenting banquets, where we advance knowledge and build excitement for the promise of the future.

Now, with the further expectation that you and Sandra are adding about my dissertation, I want my thesis to be in line with the best and newest in astronomy, brain science, psychology, self-development, real-time positive living, and education. The parenting banquets will be a kind of test. The thesis I write must stand the test of being credible with the best knowledge and dreams we have for our time in history. These speakers will help me test that while I write. Like Granddad Kelly said in his farm metaphor, buckets must hold water."

Dr. Logan responded in his usual confident manner and with a request. "Steve, I am sure your bucket will hold water, and when you complete your dissertation, may I have the privilege of being among the first to read it?"

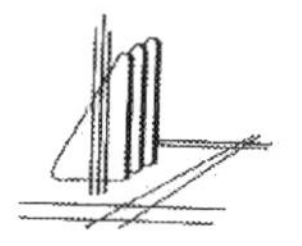

Chapter Six

Special Announcement! Parenting in A Partnership With Children

"That is the house of dreams parents can paint!"

It was an exhilarating experience for the parents in Alpine who were gathering at the World Citizen Center for the parenting conference.

As they left the tree-spaced parking lot, they could look up in admiration at the magnificent classic structure on the crest of the hill. The long profile, with its three steel monolithic triangles and pylons that stood at the left of the main entrance, created both a sense of elegance and openness - as a place for creating future ideas and vision. It was a symbol for leading-edge identity for new tomorrows. Just walking up the walkway and onto the long welcoming patio, created a sense of being a part of something important. The atrium, with its series of skylights, extending the full length in front of the banquet hall, gave those who were gathering a sense of being in a place where the power of great ideas was leading the way as a reach for a better tomorrow. Going into the James Kelly Banquet Hall, along with one hundred other parents, created an elevated sense of expectation. The white tablecloths on the array of round tables, set with sparkling glasses and dinnerware, made them feel they were special to be included in the launch event of the Parenting Conference.

Following the special banquet dinner, quietness quickly moved across the large gathering of people seated in the Kelly Banquet Hall when Dr. Sandra stepped onto the platform, followed by Dr. David Logan and Steve Kelly who proceeded to take a seat in two of the three chairs placed just behind the speakers podium, while Dr. Sandra went to the lectern, and said, "Before we begin this celebration program you get to hear a very special announcement. As minister of the World Citizen Church I have the privilege of inviting Dr. David Logan to come and make that special announcement."

Dr. Logan approached the lectern with excitement. He began immediately. "Before we celebrate a dream by opening the conference on Parents In A Partnership With Children, we have a high privileged of celebrating another dream.

One day as Steve Kelly, Dr. Sandra Kelly, and I were meeting on the deck of my retreat cottage on the peaks of Eagles View Mountain to talk about the creation of a parenting conference, I went over to the edge of the deck and leaned against the rail, overlooking Alpine. Then I turned and said, 'Steve, something else needs to have your attention at the same time we are planning the Parenting Conference. You need to make room in your work to complete your dissertation for your doctoral degree. Unless you move that part of your dream forward to completion, it will become a limiting ceiling on the great potential you have for leadership. You need the knowledge that new quest will add to your story, and the title that helps people recognize your level of knowledge, skills, and leadership. Besides that, I know it was your granddad's dream for you. I know it's a dream that Sandra has for you. And it's one I hold for you and your extended service to the World Citizen Center. It will give you a larger place in whatever your future story may be.'

Steve has followed that dream. He spent many hours up at my cottage on Eagles View, while he wrote his dissertation. When it was completed and presented before his dissertation committee at the university, it won their full approval. So, I am now privileged to hold in my hand a very special document, which is an important milestone for Steve Kelly. Of course, it's an important milestone for us here in Alpine and for the World Citizen Center. This is the day we get to celebrate that achievement, along with Steve!"

Then, as though he were lifting a torch like Lady Liberty, Dr. Logan held the bound volume of Steve's dissertation up with pride, and said, "This is a copy of Dr. Steve Kelly's dissertation entitled, *TOTAL ENVIRONMENT, Pathways for New Tomorrows!* Upon the completion of this important document, Steve has now been awarded the degree of Doctor of Philosophy in Environmental Science."

The audience didn't wait. Immediately they stood to their feet in an extended applause. When the people were finally seated again, Dr. Logan said, "To us here in Alpine it is more than a degree awarded by his university, it is a degree in world citizenship, earned right here in Alpine where the now, Dr. Steve Kelly, has been the key leader in creating the World Citizen Center. Your applause shows how much you appreciate his leadership. Steve Kelly is like a son to me. Sandra is like a daughter to me. Steve and Sandra are among Alpine's most esteemed citizens!" Immediately there was another enthusiastic applause.

Before Dr. Steve Kelly opens this Parenting Conference, I want to ask him to come and talk about the dissertation that the committee approved, for which he has been awarded his Ph D degree. So, Dr. Steve Kelly - I like the sound of that - Dr. Steve

Kelly, would you come now and share with us some ideas from your dissertation."

When Steve came to the stage amid another round of applause, he was greeted by Dr. Logan, with a firm handshake, and then with an arm around Steve's shoulder, as an extra expression of his esteem.

Steve began by saying, "Thank you, Dr. Logan, for all you have done to make this moment possible. And, Thank You, Sandra, for your cooperative support. And thanks to the many people here who have helped to make this story possible.

Essentially, my dissertation is a story. It's the story of World Citizen Church and it's distinguished minister, Dr. Sandra Kelly, now my beloved wife. It is the story of people who changed the name of their church from Grovemont Church to World Citizen Church with an accompanying identity of world citizenship. It's the story of a church that dared to put an icon of the Master Teacher at the center of its worship and identity. It's the story of Dr. David Logan, whose acute disappointment with tradition and backward looking paradigms for worship, led him on a search for a more open-ended faith, based in knowledge and the hope of building a better tomorrow. Dr. David Logan's personal and financial commitment to a new dream has led to the vision that has now become the World Citizen Center. All this is in my story dissertation.

It's the story that began with the faith and philosophy of my granddad, Dr. James Kelly. It was his philosophy of life and commitment to a knowledge-based faith that, while it may have reflections from the past, must always be about the future! In the long progression of the human story, with both its failures and its successes, we have arrived at our remarkable moment in time when we must have a new respect for our potential in our total environment of which we are a part. It brings us all to a place in the story where we can dream our best dreams that launch us into our greatest new tomorrows. It's the story of the long progression of the human family from the cave age to the digital age, where our opportunity is to make the future better than the past. While our place in the story is only for a brief moment, that moment is of immense importance. It is our link in the story that connects the unfinished dreams from yesterday, to sunrise dreams for our greatest tomorrows.

Those dreams have a new focus in the World Citizen Center. It's here we have the opportunity to be a part of that unfinished dream as we move forward by making the Big Ten Universal Qualities central in the continuing story. It's here that each of us can give our best dreams their best chance to happen! But it's time for us to launch a new program for our World Citizen Center and to focus on the increasing importance of parents as teachers. So, welcome parents! The future is in our hands! We are shapers of the future!

Being a parent in a partnership with your children is one of the most important things you will ever do. Your home is one of the most important learning centers of the world. Whether it's a place for five or six people, or only two or three, when you make your home a place where the Big Ten Universal Qualities are taught by your words and your example, that will be a place of dreams and sunrise beginnings! It will fulfill the dream of the person whose books inspired the World Citizen Center. Dr. James Kelly said, "I have a dream that the Big Ten Universal Qualities will be taught in the learning centers of all the world." You can make your home into one of those learning centers where the Big Ten Universal Qualities are taught by parents!

To see that picture, step back with me into a story from yesterday that was not quite like that. In fact, not like that at all .

A sense of despair was written on Charlene's face and in her body language as she got on the school bus that morning. Charlene is not her real name. In my own school bus days, I was already on that school bus when I saw her as she stepped on quickly. Her face was flat. Not literally, but in terms of expression, it was empty. Her lifeless emotions indicated that she had just walked out of a home where conflict and fear pervaded the atmosphere, and had already washed the energy of hope and joy right out of the beginning of a new day.

I knew her parents. They were not happy people. It was as though they were hoarding life and holding on to it as something to protect and keep from losing, rather than something they could give away like the joy of the sunshine. It was like they were afraid to give their best to life, lest they not get the best in return, when, in fact, just the opposite is true, even as the Master Teacher said, 'give and gifts will be given to you.' So, instead of Charlene being light hearted and skipping out of the house and bounding on the school bus as a new adventure in the wonders of learning and a time to be with new friends, she seemed so sad. Her face seemed to be telling a story that said, 'I had no fun at home this morning. My parents were not even trying to make life fun. It's as though they lived in the same house, but they were not friends together. It's like they were afraid to trust life - afraid to let happiness define the unique and special moments of being a young family. Instead of living in a wonderful world of discovery, with the high privilege of being a family in this great time in history, they were just making a living, and protecting themselves and their children against dangers that may be hidden in each new day. All those things showed on Charlene's face as she boarded the bus, clamored down the aisle with a frozen expression, and sat down. Instead of speaking to anyone, she didn't even look at a single person. She just found an empty seat and sat down, alone, stolid, and somber, with the weight of disappointment pushing down on her dreams. No big dreams were in her eyes, awakening the energy of vision and hope. There was no sunrise in her spirit.

If what Charlene represented were a color, everything would be painted gray. No sunshine yellow, no sky blue, no green like the grass, just gray. No words like those Oliver sang as he greeted a new day, with wonder and excitement, 'Who will buy this wonderful morning … what am I to do to keep the sky so blue?'

Could Charlene's picture have been different? Maybe. And, if Charlene represents any of us, as we board the school buses of life, do we need to get out our paint brush and repaint? Can we use a new color chart of dynamic words of hope and promise, with no gray in it?

To repaint, first, we will need to add a generous splash of the color of kindness and caring. We can paint the walls with honesty and respect to radiate a spirit of giving and generosity. We can paint the dark corners with the freedom of openness and trust, so we can collaborate together with tolerance, fairness, and integrity. Then we can add the uplifting colors of diplomacy and nobility to give our new rainbow colors a sense of the high privilege we have to live out simple goodness. And, let's open the shades and let in the sunlight of joy. Not tomorrow, but today! Parents are the artists of that kind of future. Parents can paint the world with the dreams of wonder and hope. Children will love it!

As parents, when we send 'Charlene' out to get on the school bus, we can let her go out the door, dancing with dreams that are energized by positive emotions. You may already have figured it out. I am talking about being parents who create a positive atmosphere at home by living out the word colors of the Big Ten Universal Qualities. Of course, you can't get that kind of paint out of a can. It comes out of the great ideas and dreams we can paint into our own identity when we reach for the best we can be. Then we can paint that picture with the identity sunlight colors of joy and confidence, so that Charlene, and thousands of little girls and boys in the world like her, can get on the school bus of life singing with Oliver, 'Who will buy this beautiful morning … what am I to do to keep the sky so blue?'

Parents have that kind of opportunity and high privilege! The uplifting, creative, inspiring word colors of the Big Ten Universal Qualities can be painted on any home. Be it a cottage or castle, be it a mobile home or an apartment, that home can be painted with a surging energy that announces that the people living in that house are giving their best to life as their request of life. That is the house of dreams parents can paint!"

Steve shifted his tone from painting a dream to offering a privilege. "You will be very pleased by the speaker who has been chosen to launch the opening of this Parenting Partnership conference, where the focus is on parenting in a partnership with children. Once you hear this distinguished lady, you will realize how right it is that we begin by seeing our place in the story in terms of where we are in a far larger story.

Our speaker is an astronomer who will help us see our place in the endless story of the cosmos, where we take our place in the Milky Way Galaxy as one of millions of galaxies, and where we have a place on one of the Milky Way's little planets called Earth. It's here on our little planet that we have the high privilege of being parents in our moment of time. Are there more planets like ours? We are eager to find out. But in the meantime, we know this is a very important planet. It's our home - our place to reach for our dreams. This little planet is our home where we get to live out our story in our time in the history.

One of the interesting and delightful persons who can help us see our place in that story is our speaker. She is on the faculty of our Sagan University, and one of the world's distinguished astronomers!

So, I now have the honor and privilege of inviting Dr. Arnetta Segal to this World Citizen Center stage, to open our conference on Parenting in a Partnership with Children.

Dr. Arnetta Segal moved to the podium with her head down slightly. When she lifted it she began to sing calmly.

> Twinkle, twinkle, little star,
> How I wonder what you are!
> Up above the world so high,
> Like a diamond in the sky.

Even if that's not great singing, it is good poetry. It is good astronomy. And it is good parenting. It is good parenting because you sang that lullaby to your baby while that marvel of all existence was nestled in your arms, drifting off into sleep. I sang it to Billy before he got to be that curious and energetic two year-old. Now we stack blocks but still are in the arena of mystery. What holds one block on top of another, and then another until they get tall and begin to topple because Billy knocks them down just to see them fall. What makes them fall? What makes a lot of things as they are? What makes a star twinkle?

We don't wonder about stars as much as we did in the earlier days of human curiosity about what's out there. Now we see them through the amazing telescopes like Hubble, and soon, Kepler - those units that combine science, technology, and engineering into spectacular instruments of discovery.

As Steve said, I am astronomer. I study stars, and other things which are out there. In the meantime, I not only marvel at what's out there, I marvel at what's here, in a very special place in the universe - in all existence. In our cosmos, here is so far away from there, that we measure in light years - in millions of light years.

Is our planet alone in all this space? Our answer to that question may be revealed with the help of our continuing explorations of what is out there. Even if we do discover other worlds like ours, that does not distract from the Earth's very special and unique story. Our planet home is very, very special. So, I not only look through telescopes and marvel at out there, but I look at where we are and marvel as the wonders of the earth.

But what a beautiful little poem Jane Taylor wrote about both places. Her poem continues in five verses, one more of which I want to quote instead of singing.

> When the blazing sun is set,
> When the grass with dew is wet,
> Then you show your little light,
> Twinkle, twinkle, all the night.

The darkness helps to reveal where we are.

I was asked to go with a Boy Scout troop far out into a secluded place one night to talk to them as they looked up at the stars through a telescope. They are not as powerful as the ones I am privileged to use in my studies and work, but they are really very good as a result of continuing developments of technology.

We had to get away from the glow of city lights, even from the invasion of yard lights out in the country. As the scouts peered through the lens at those distant units of energy, I talked to them about where we are as seen from our observation post here on one of the other units of almost unlimited space. Our little planet so small in such a grand cosmos that it might not get any attention at all if it were not our home as the human family. So, I not only talked about where we are, but I talked about who we are. And that's what I want to do now - to talk about both where we are, then to talk about who we are.

We are a part of what may be an endless arena of existence. We are a part of galaxies, millions and millions of stars in clusters. We are a part of the Milky Way Galaxy. In that galaxy we are far out on the edge of it and part of a little solar system where the earth is one of the planets that rotate around a star - what we call the sun.

Musical artists romanticize about our rotating along with other planets and sing.

> Fly me to the moon,
> And let me play among the stars.
> Let me see what spring is like
> On jupiter and mars.

They are romanticizing about love, but of course, there is no spring on Jupiter and Mars. They don't have what we have on our unique planet, earth.

Spring is a word that belongs to Earth, where we have spring and all that makes this a place where we have blue skies and trees, streams and lakes, possible only because we are in a Goldilocks orbit around our sun.

There is a mythological story about a place like that - a Garden of Eden in which two people lived. Or course, as the story goes, they had to move out of that garden and go plant a garden of their own. But even in their new garden they still had the marvels of sunshine and rain, air and soil, and - that marvelous liquid called water, and all the marvels of springtime. It's where they had to plant their own garden - a new garden because they were no longer welcome in the old garden. But what a wonder! Outside Eden they still had all the wonders of Mother nature - all that makes earth such a special place in the expansive cosmos.

Don't begin asking too many questions, like where they got the seed, etc. - just see it as metaphorical story, then fast forward to way down here to our time in history, where we get to start new gardens which are possible because of where we are, with springtime.

I have a garden. But, I have to admit that I don't have a garden in the sense that many of you may have a productive garden of vegetables or flowers. However, I do have four tomato plants. I know that doesn't come anywhere near to ranking me with Adam and Eve's new garden, or with your garden.

Even so, what I did do, early this spring was to take a few tiny little tomato seeds and plant them in a planter. I made sure they had access to light from that little star we circle around each year, and where we spin round each day. I watched as those little seeds pushed up two tiny leaves. I watched them daily as they grew large enough to transplant into larger planters. In time they grew big and bloomed with little yellow flowers, then put on little green tomatoes. Each day I put on some of that miracle fluid that is so special on earth – I put on them, the same fluid as Adam and Eve depended on for their garden. Each day I watched those little tomatoes as a shadow of pink appeared. Finally, they turned red and were ready for harvest. As you know, inside each of my precious tomatoes there were dozens of little seeds, ready for a new beginning in another garden.

What I just don't understand is what makes the seeds want to grow. And I don't understand why anything wants to be. Nor do I understand why atoms want to be atoms, and why the electrons, protons, and neutrons furiously race about each other, working together year after year, century after century, millions upon millions of years. They don't even seem to get tired of wanting to be the working dynamics of molecular existence. But, in my four tomato plants, and in the stars millions of light years away, the elements of all existence never seem to get tired of wanting to be. I just don't know why anything wants to exist, here on earth, or in the remotest parts of the cosmos. So, I live in amazement at what I see as I look through the marvelous telescopes of our time at the endless splendor of things that keep on wanting to be. All this makes me marvel at where we are.

But the more I learn about where we are makes marvel at who we are. Who is that baby we sing lullabies to? Who are the parents who sit on the floor and stack blocks with a little two-year-old boy? What guidelines do we have to help us to be partners with our children?

Steve asked me to read Dr. James Kelly's books before I came to speak to you. I did that. And the more I read, the more I turned the telescope of my mind toward those words which recur again and again - words that can be chosen to help us guide who we are - The Big Ten Universal Qualities.

Yes, we are a part of the cosmos. And it is a part of us. Atoms and molecules, just like the stars, but what else? Who are we?

There is so much I don't know, or that any of us know. So, more than ever I am engaged in not only where we are, but what we can learn about who we are. And that quest is so very important in our digital-information-molecular age. And what I think is that the search for who we are is something very sacred. I live amid the marvel of the sacred!

In our time, we get to work with the greatest tools we ever held in our hands, and we get to work with the greatest thing on earth - our children. And I don't know enough about raising children to talk to you about it. Who does? Still we have to learn what we can and share it as best we can. I could learn a lot from so many of you about how to be a partner with two-year-old Billy now and as he grows older. But I am finding lots of help from Dr. Kelly's books. I am eager to learn how to live by the Big Ten Universal Qualities and how to help Billy learn them.

Dr. Kelly thinks our home should be one of the learning centers of the world where the Big Ten qualities are taught. And what the World Citizen Center is emphasizing in this Parenting Conference is that we are to make our home one of those places. I am a parent and learning along with you as parents how to be in a partnership with our children. It's where I am eager to learn how to live out the Big Ten Universal Qualities. We have two more of these banquet events and my husband and I will be here to learn all we can.

I am already sold on the thesis - that children grow best when they learn the words of the Big Ten Universal Qualities. And where can they learn them? The rest of that thesis is that parents can also learn those important words, model them in their own story, and be the teachers who teach them to their children.

Kindness and caring are two of those words. All children need to experience kindness from their parents. That need never stops. We are always parents to our children. I am new to being Billy's mother, but when I reflect on my own childhood, I know how important kindness and caring can be. I want Billy to have that kind of memories.

Respect. That's one of the words that reach down across the years. Respect is such a two way street. To be respected, we have to give respect away, especially to our children.

Then there is the summit word of the Big Ten - nobility. It links with that often repeated phrase, *noblesse* oblige - nobility obligates. It's about privilege and our responsibility that goes with it. It's what we have as those who are privileged to be parents. And to be what we need to be as partners with our children we need the guidance of a star - a guiding set of words that define who we are and can be - the Big Ten.

It was Dr. Kelly's dream that the qualities of the Big Ten be taught in all the learning centers of the world. The goal of these Parenting Conference is to help us make our home one of those learning center. My husband and I will make our home one of those centers.

The words of the Big Ten Universal Qualities have made me see my world in a different way. More than I have ever realized before the Big Ten words are vital in our identity framework. More than ever I believe we need the Big Ten words as a guiding identity star.

When the blazing sun is set,
When the grass with dew is wet,
Then you show your little light,
Twinkle, twinkle, all the night.

Then the traveler in the dark
Thanks you for your tiny spark,
We could not see where to go
If you did not twinkle so.

As your bright and tiny spark
Lights the traveler in the dark,
Though I know not what you are,
Twinkle, twinkle, little star.

Good night, fellow parents and partners with our children.

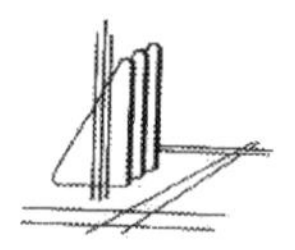

Chapter Seven

A Picture of Ourselves

"Americans want optimists to lead them."
Martin E. P. Seligman

Dr. Sandra stepped up to the speaker's lectern and said, "Welcome to the second exciting Parenting Conference. Steve asked me if I would be willing to present our speaker this evening because he is one of the members of the World Citizen Church, where I am privileged to serve as minister.

Our speaker is a psychologist here in Alpine and a distinguished professor at Sagan University. Having taught and served here in Alpine for twelve years, he needs little introduction. But I want to say that, along with his distinguishing academic credentials, he is a generous and caring person, highly respected by his fellow members at the church and by the people of Alpine. So, with great respect, I present to you our friend and distinguished psychologist, Dr. Vernon Lucas."

When Dr. Lucas walked onto the platform, with his obvious limp, he stood behind the lectern, swept his gaze across the audience with a pleasant smile and simply began in his always friendly tone of voice.

"It is a privilege and a big challenge to speak about parenting to fellow parents from the perspective of a psychologist. Therefore, I have had to put a big question to myself. 'Does a psychologist have a better handle on how to be a good parent than others?' This question sent me back to the drawing board in search of answers. I went to a book by a psychologist who, earlier, was head of the American Psychological Association, Martin E. P. Seligman. In his book, *Learned Optimism*, he says, "Life inflicts the same setbacks and tragedies on the optimist as on the pessimist, but the optimist weathers them better. As we have seen, the optimist bounces back from defeat, and, with his life somewhat poorer, he picks up and starts again." Then Dr. Seligman says, "Americans want optimists to lead them."[2]

I believe children want to be led by optimists. I have learned anew that the skills we need so much to be both a positive optimist, and to be our best as parents, are defined in the Big Ten Universal Qualities.

Steve wanted me to tell my story. My life began with a story that is different. You can see this slump in one of my shoulders, and you can't help but to have noticed my significant limp as I walked on stage. It's not new, or even recent. I was born with it. It was severe enough that it limited what I could do as a boy. No baseball. No basketball. Nobody wanted me on a cheerleading squad, not with a shoulder like this. And those glasses - I have now traded them for contact lens, but as a boy, I had to wear thick glasses, so I was afraid that no girl would ever look at me twice.

But what I had, was parents who took that word 'handicapped' and turned it around! They said, 'Now, remember son, if what you have, is all you have, it's up to you to make the best of it. So, what's not out of shape, and what's not handicapped, is your brain.

[2] Martin E. P. Seligman. *Learned Optimism*.

You have what we gave you through your genes, but that's not set in concrete. What you also have is a brain that is ready for you to, set and reset, to guide and shape your life for a great future. So, what you get to do is to tell your brain what you want from a life. You can send your brain a picture of yourself as a winner in spite of challenges. You get to tell it to lead you by your positive assets which are not defined by your limitations. Those assets are almost unlimited. You can choose who you want to be in your story, and your brain will guide you to that story. That's sacred.'

My wise parents asked me to look beyond my difficulties for unfolding opportunities. That approach didn't make a lot of sense to me in high school, but it did make enough sense that when I brought my report card home and showed it to my parents they beamed with pride. All A's. Out of that level of achievement, one of my teachers encouraged me to apply for a college scholarship. My dad was a carpenter and my mother was a stay-at-home-mom. They never could have afforded to send me to college. So, when I applied and won a scholarship, it was a re-launch to another planet. I still had my limp and my disfigured shoulder and my limited eyesight. But when I took a class in psychology, I moved into another orbit. I was hooked. I began to think that my being handicapped could serendipitously help me to help others with their disabilities, visible or hidden. After college, I went for the degrees I needed to be a psychologist. So now I am both a practicing psychologist and a teacher. Being a teacher is at the height of my dreams. It's who I am, handicaps and all. Using my own story as an example, I tell people to look beyond their handicaps and turn struggle into opportunity.

Steve wanted me to tell my story in a reference to parents being in a partnership with their children. My parents did that. They helped me to self-design - to learn on my own, how to steer my way. Good parents do that. They don't own their children. They don't abuse their children's bodies, especially not their minds. Instead, they nurture the ability to develop an identity of dignity and worth beyond whatever limitations are unique to their places in the story.

Girls. My assumptions about girls changed when I was in grad school. I found a girl who saw beyond my thick glasses and stooped shoulder. And that girl became my wife and the mother of our three children and one of the best mothers one could have. Talk about someone I admire so greatly, she's that person. And talk about someone putting the best of the Big Ten qualities into one's story, my wife does that, and my parents did that. No, my parents had never heard these words clustered together into what we now know of as the Big Ten Universal Qualities, but they lived those words. I am the fortunate beneficiary of that, and I am trying to do that, too, and now as never before.

Steve asked me to read all of Dr. Kelly's books. I had already read them as part of our special reading program at the church, but I did what he asked, I read them again. And guess what focused anew, like a new rainbow in the sky? It was Dr. Kelly's Big Ten Universal Qualities. Those ten words are like a GPS for identity. They are a condensation of learned optimism into a cluster of power words we can send to our brain with a request that the brain send signals right back as a positive guide to make those ten qualities real in our own story. It's like Dr. Kelly says so often in his writings, give our best dreams their best chance to happen.

My parents had their own way of applying those principles. They said, 'Son, don't let your handicaps lead your story. Instead, find your way to detour around them - to negate their effects on your bigger and more important goals, so that you can render your handicaps as inconsequential to achieving your goals. Redirect. Reset the mind. Write a great new story in spite of them. Set goals that refuse to stop at handicaps.' What amazing parents I had. As you can tell, I have used some of my own language in restating what they said, but as a capsule, they helped me to shape my own identity. And now, here I am. And the story goes on.

Talk about being a learner, I am one of the biggest learners in this Parenting Conference program. I listened as our previous speaker talked about the new insights she gained from reading Dr. Kelly's books. What all this has done for me is to set a whole new level of insight into shaping and reshaping personality.

In the long and slow progressions in the human story, there was a big step up from the age of the cave man, with sticks-and-stones tools, to the age of bronze and dwelling houses. Then, age after age, across the centuries, the human family has stepped up again and again. We stepped up when Galileo, with his improved telescope, helped us learn that our earth was not the center of our solar system. In turn, we have gone through a series of paradigms about who we are and can be.

Nearer to our time, we took a step up from Freudian psychology, from blaming our problems on our parent-child conflicts. Then we stepped up again when we saw the power that positive thinking can have on our self-understanding and success. Now we are learning that some of the emotions we struggle with, have a specific location in the brain where, more and more, we can change them for new levels of health. We have taken another step up in positive psychology in which we are learning new ways to build on our strengths. We are also learning to reroute brain activity to detour around some malfunctions to create new pathways for guidance.

In psychology we do analysis and diagnosis, but that is never enough. We must have guiding identity markers that refocus the future. I often work with people who are always analyzing the past instead of shaping the future. That's backward. We need guidance from the future as engineered out of our growing knowledge and our best dreams. In short, we need updated versions of the kingdom of heaven vision the Master Teacher talked about - where we give and gifts will come back to us - where we give our best to life as our request of life.

Now, as a psychologist, what about those ten words? They can be important healing words, and therapeutic identity markers. I want to assure you that I am acutely aware that some people have such deep emotional and psychological problems, they require specialized treatment by professionals in intense counseling and therapy. But, as part of that rebuilding process, the Big Ten qualities can help. Almost everyone can experience valuable healing of their identity just by making the Big Ten their own chosen identity framework. That's why I make Dr. Kelly's books available in my office. I'll say more about that later.

In his book, *The Future We Ask For,* Dr. Kelly lists Ten Principles of Problem Solving. One principle of great importance, is Dr. Kelly's advice about living beyond our problems. He says, "*Some problems will never go away. Some are not in your control. The only choice you have is to adjust to them, and keep on adjusting, learn from them, detour around, live triumphantly with and beyond them, and succeed in spite of them. You can't change the past, but the future is still open. Figure out the best way to go on from here. There are positive ways to deal with negative situations. In short, learn to make the best of the worst, and the most of the least.*"

So the opportunity to be the very best we can be is always at hand - to make whatever our station in life, chosen or un-chosen, into opportunity.

There are many parents who are caught in very special circumstances. Children born with disabilities, injury from accidents, medical factors, etc. That's where we are challenged to learn all over again as parents. We are challenged to make the best of alternatives. These are the people who come to me for help. We are challenged together and we fall back on resources available. I often prescribe reading Dr. Kelly's books, especially the book, *The Future We Ask For,* in which all ten of the principles of problem solving are defined in down to earth terms.

Let me highlight another one of those ten principles. It's the one about making mistakes. We all make them. Nobody is perfect. So what are we to do? Dr. Kelly says for us to make sure we are working on the future instead of merely fretting about the past. He says, *When things get broken, fix them, if possible, or wise, then move on to make new beginnings beyond old endings. Put the past behind you and the future before you, just as much as you possibly can. All mistakes are not catastrophic. So, don't just live with your mistakes, live beyond them. Take hold of the future!*

I want to make sure you don't overlook the last principle Dr. Kelly talks about in his book. It's the one about our best life being an ongoing process. It's while we are out there trying our best that the doors keep opening. Let me read part of it. *Keep your best dreams alive. Keep trying. Do not give up on worthy goals. We win only if we are still in there playing the game. Reflect on yesterday, but envision tomorrow. Trust the positive, energizing, dynamic set forth in the dependable axiom of Jesus, "While you are asking, it will be given you; while you are seeking, you will find; and while you are knocking, it will be opened to you." (Matt. 7:7 Literal translation from Greek)*

Here's a promise I can make to you. If you will make the Big Ten universal qualities and the Ten Principles of Problem Solving into an integral part of your identity network and just keep on trying and never give up on them, they will release an adrenalin boost to your emotions and make you into a far healthier person, and more successful in your career and family relationships.

So, what you can do is, respect your spouse, respect your children. If you were meeting the president of your country, wouldn't you try to be your best? Give that kind of up-reach and respect to each other in your family network. Sometimes that's easy, sometimes its not, but the payoff is big. You will like yourself better, and others will like you better!

The handicap, under which I lived from my childhood, tended to make me ready to live a little more on the trial-and-error edge - to test outcomes. It may be that the Big Ten could be put into clinical trials in research settings to test results. But what is known already is that, all of us can test our own anecdotal evidence, and be eager to tell about it - that the Big Ten Universal Qualities work! They bring positive change into our story.

I decided to do a question and answer anecdotal survey. It's not a scientific test, only an anecdotal test, but it has a lot to say about our own story in which we are choosers and learners.

I asked twenty students to read a selection from Dr. Kelly's books in which he talks about the Big Ten. I asked them if they would try to incorporate the Big Ten identity markers into their identity base, along with whatever other identities they have. I assured them it was part of an experiment. I didn't need to push. They were ready to enter into the experiment. I didn't want to structure it too much, so I asked them just to apply the Big Ten qualities in their own unique ways.

Four weeks later, I asked them to complete a survey with questions about any changes in their relationships with their professors, fellow students, college administration, parents, and friends and to note changes in their outlook on life. Their responses were very positive. Most students reported an increased sense of self-confidence and inner attitudes. They reported that they were less conflicted and more positive. Most reported that they were more respectful of their professors. I liked that. They reported that they were being more tolerant of others. Their outlook on life was more open and hopeful. Their results were positive, and most of them indicated that they would continue the Big Ten identity markers as a personal choice.

Their positive expectations of themselves moved up as a kind of self-fulfillment. My premise that the Big Ten identity markers were indeed aligned with the best of psychology was supported by anecdotal evidence. I am ready to make this a part of my classes each future semester.

What is open for continued study is, what the effect the Big Ten can have on the health of the mind and emotions - on our psychological health. I believe these universal qualities help people feel more confident about their identity and persona.

Number one, these qualities compliment collaboration and diplomacy at home, school, work, and in social settings. That's a big step forward.

Number two, they have a healing effect on destructive and

conflicting emotions of anger, resentment, and fear, in such a way that these negative emotions no longer lead the response people make to many of life's challenges and frustrations.

Number three, they create a 'checks and balances' on our choices so that, we not only reach for these qualities, but measure by them as a corrective activity of our minds and emotions.

I await to see if major centers for medicine take up the Big Ten Universal Qualities as a definitive part of wholeness. The test would be a measure of how well these qualities play over into our physical and emotional health. It would test to see if these qualities build new levels of fun and happiness into family life.

So what about the choice to go for quality in relationships?

Sometimes a young person can go terribly wrong, when actually there has been nothing wrong with their genetics or their parental relationships, just that they chose the wrong friends and influences. They did not choose the identity markers that make for a good life. That's when it is time for a reset - time to turn failure upside down - time for a turning point, and that's not always easy. That's when they get referred to me. Life can never be as good as it could have been, had they chosen the Big Ten guiding qualities, but still there can be very positive resets for new tomorrows.

Sometimes psychiatry and psychology can help people turn around. And sometimes religion, informed by a knowledge-based faith, can be an effective turning point influence. And always, knowing the power of the Big Ten identity markers, can lead in important new directions. That's why I want all my patients and my students to know about the Big Ten.

What we do know is that the Big Ten words are healthy words and they can guide us down the best roads of life. And they are healing words that help any of us find new beginnings beyond old endings.

My profession is about helping people take a new direction. The way back may be long and difficult, but good parents can make a positive difference. Parenting never stops. Those who get caught up in the swift currents of destructive choices will find that the Big Ten qualities can help them turn their story around.

Sometimes the reach needs to be a second reach, or a third reach for a new beginning. And sometimes parents may need to help their children reach again beyond broken emotions, and failed dreams. Successful, winning parenting never stops. The need goes on to be supportive and caring in our relationships, honest and respectful of our children's need to be learners out of life experience, both good and bad. Whatever is down the road of life, the wonderful, supportive, caring, collaborative goals of being good parents do not end. Partnership goes right on for the long haul with our children.

The better parents do in living by the Big Ten, the less their children will need to come to me for what I can do for them. So, I am discovering anew that one of the best things I can do for people is to point them to the Big Ten qualities and ask them to make them a part of the dynamics of their working identity day after day, hour after hour in a reach for a healthy identity and life.

In an article in Psychology Today, "Motivation is Contagious", Ron Friedman said, "The more people we see expressing a particular feeling, the more likely we are to adopt it ourselves, amplifying it in the process." He reported on research he and his colleagues conducted at the University of Rochester, and found that "simply placing participants in the same room as a highly motivated individual improved their drive and improved their performance.[3]

When I was invited to speak at this Parenting Conference series, Steve personally came out to my office at the university, and talked about the objectives of the program in terms of its spreading influence here in Alpine and beyond. He said, 'I hope you will adopt the Big Ten universal qualities personally, and as a family." He explained that the hope was that many people in Alpine would

[3] Psychology Today. April 2013

adopt these qualities at such a level of interest that others will see what a difference these qualities can make and will also adopt them for their own family relationships. He said there would be no attempt to make this into a clinical trial, only that people become a test in their own story. We don't want to promote it as some new program, parallel to weight loss programs, so much as to let it be a natural promotion, a kind of contagious influence for good that goes on and on as an unconscious positive energy.'

Steve's invitation expanded and became personal. He said, 'Vernon, we want you to come and speak, but beyond that, we hope you will try living by the Big Ten in your own unique ways in your profession.' What I understand is that Steve went to the other speakers with the same kind of appeal. What he said to me was that he knew it was a big challenge, but that nothing happens until we try. That's when he began to quote from Edgar A Guest's poem.

> Somebody said that it couldn't be done,
> But he with a chuckle replied
> That "maybe it couldn't," but he would be one
> Who wouldn't say so till he'd tried.
> So he buckled right in with the trace of a grin
> On his face. If he worried he hid it.
> He started to sing as he tackled the thing
> That couldn't be done, and he did it.[4]

That poem is about risking. It's about going beyond the safety zones, about what happens while we are trying our best to reach challenging goals. He hoped I would try the Big Ten and then talk about that. His appeal was personal. I couldn't turn him down. But more than that, I wanted to try the Big Ten Universal Qualities. I wanted to do my own test. I wanted to see how this set of qualities could work in my own story and career. So, I have been doing my

[4] Edgar A Guest

own testing. I have been getting some of my patients to try the Big Ten. The stories they are telling are positive. What I am discovering is that it is working in my own family relationships. We are less defensive, more confident and relaxed, and having much more fun. That in itself is a winner.

Is it contagious? I think it is. But it's a good contagion. I can't name names, but one person, who has tried the Big Ten, said, 'The best result is that I can feel it. I feel different inside. I am less hostile and defensive, more ready to be tolerant. It's like it is a framework in which one quality supports the others. It's like, if you are kind, you have also expanded your ability to be diplomatic and more respectful of others.'

I not only liked what I was hearing from others about the positive results, but I found the same changes in my own experience. I like the new me.

And, that's my story. Steve wanted us to align our careers with our stories, and that leads me to tell you about a new part of my story. I was in college when I got interested in psychology, I knew I wanted to help people find that kind of inner healing that makes people more confident as a part of their growth and healing. And now, in the Big Ten, I think we have something that is worth sharing in and through our professions.

So here is what I am trying to do to expand this kind of influence. If you come by my office, you will find copies of Dr. Kelly's books on the tables along with the magazines. And near the checkout window you will see a little bookcase with copies of the books available for any patient who wants to purchase copies for themselves. Our staff will simply add them to their bill, without it being a part of their insurance.

Why? I am becoming aware that our most positive thoughts and emotions are awakened when we choose to live out the Big Ten qualities. They just make us better people, more positive and confident, less defensive and more tolerant. They increase our diplomatic and networking skills. We become more ready to look for the good in others and less likely to criticize. We just feel better inside, more wholesome and more at home with ourselves. We like ourselves better, and in turn, others like us better. The rewards and benefits of the Big Ten make us more successful in our careers and in life.

All of this is the reason I am now making Dr. Kelly's books supplementary reading for my students. And, sometimes I simply write a prescriptions in which I ask a patient to read these healing books.

I have personally tried Dr. Kelly's One A Day Identity Vitamins. Some people may think it is just to simple to work. But it does work. People who will choose one of the Big Ten qualities as their word for the day, and try to measure by and live up to it will find that this changes their future for the better. The change won't happen overnight, but over time, choosing our One A Day Identity vitamin will make us into better persons! They will rewrite the software of identity until it signals new beginnings beyond old endings.

Some people who seek my counsel have nothing seriously wrong with them. But they are restless, and seeking to satisfy their inner hungers. A lot of those hungers would be satisfied if they only made the Big Ten Universal Qualities the identity markers central in their stories.

Some children's maladies are deeply entrenched, but many are not, and will go away if their parents live out the Big Ten qualities as the atmosphere they create in the home. Healing of attitudes will occur. Relationships will be based more on trust than on defensive resistance. Parents can be partners with their children and make the Big Ten into words that lead the identity for a new future.

But this approach of spreading the influence of qualities-based living is not limited to psychologists. Ministers can devise their own ways of making this creative and wholesome approach a part of their ministry. They could make Dr. Kelly's books available.

They could lead discussion groups among fellow ministers, or for their own members who read Dr. Kelly's books and then share in discussion groups. Classes could create extended studies. Educators have a great opportunity to make the overarching qualities of the Big Ten into a part of how they teach and guide. The same goes for all our professions and all of us in our careers. We can be part of the spreading the influence of the Big Ten.

So you are a parent? So am I. You want to be the best parent you can be? So do I. Our children are learners. They need to learn the Big Ten Universal Qualities. And so do their parents! That makes us need to be learners in a lifetime partnership with our children. And, one more thing. It's good psychology!

And with that, let me say, Thank you for this high privilege to share with you as fellow parents.

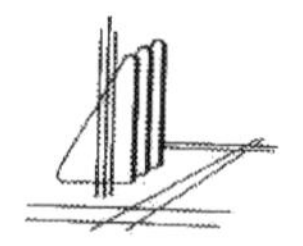

Chapter Nine

Clark and Jenny's Story

"No, I never heard them ringing at all till there was you."
"The Music Man"

THE BUZZ OF CONVERSATION AROUND THE BANQUET TABLES AT THE third Parenting Banquet was still going on when Steve walked to center stage. Instead of calling for attention he stood there and waited. One by one people became aware that he was ready to begin the session and ceased their conversation.

Instead of beginning to speak, Steve turned and watched as three persons came walking onto the stage, each one carrying a rocking chair. When they had placed two of them side by side and the other one slightly across from those two, Steve turned to the curious audience and began quietly.

"It was springtime the first time I went out to Clark and Jenny Henderson's home. Just driving along between the blossoming apple trees on each side of the long gravel drive, with grasses growing between the well packed routes, was like being transported into another world. In one minute I had entered an atmosphere created by the marvels of nature expressed in a grand apple orchard. Moments later, the farm house, apple packing shed, and farm buildings came into view. Clark and Jenny were expecting me and came out to meet me at the car and graciously greeted me. When I was invited to come and sit on the front porch with them, I knew I was in an atmosphere radiated by the warmth of Clark and Jenny's caring generosity.

Some of you have been out there to that spreading valley farm and know the feeling. And you know already the magnitude of congeniality you feel when you talk to either Clark or Jenny. They exude such a warmth and welcome that you feel it. No wonder then, when the planning committee for this Parenting Conference sat in the Eagles View Conference room, and the names of Clark and Jenny were suggested as speakers who would embody a positive representation of parenting, we all knew immediately that we needed to search no further. It was as though a kind of musical melody floated in the air with their names. And those of you who already know them will agree with our choice to invite them to be our speakers about parenting in this conference. Those of you who don't know them yet, will be glad that you have this opportunity to meet and get to know them, as they share their story.

So, what I want to do now is to invite Clark and Jenny Henderson to come to the platform and take up two of the three rocking chairs we borrowed from their front porch, with their permission, of course. We want them to occupy the two rockers that are close together and I will sit on one side and ask a few lead-in questions and then listen as they inspire all of us as they share their story. Join me now in welcoming Clark and Jenny Henderson!"

After the welcoming applause, Steve began the conversation by saying, "Thank you so much, Jenny and Clark, for giving all of us this opportunity to sit on a representation of your farmhouse porch now and share in your story.

On the one hand, this may seem like an interview in that I am going to ask a few questions, but on the other hand, it will not be like an interview at all, but like I have just sat down with you again on your front porch in open conversation, while apple blossoms flutter in the air.

Jenny, I know you are feeling the urge to ask, 'Would you like to have a glass of iced tea?' And if we were actually sitting on your front porch, the answer would be, 'Oh, yes, I would love to have some of your delicious sweet iced tea. That would be great!' Then you would be back in only moments with some of the best sweet tea anyone ever tasted. But for now, and here, let's just imagine looking down the road between the apple trees as we visit with you on the porch."

Steve continued. "Clark and Jenny, we would like to hear your story. Maybe as you tell it, we can figure out why, when I come back from visiting you, I just can't wait to tell somebody about my delightful visit. Even here now, with your relaxed manner, let me ask what it is that makes us feel such a sense that you are quietly and confidently at home with life, always so 'up' on everything? How do you account for that?"

"That's easy, Clark said immediately, "It's Jenny. Do you remember that song from "The Music Man," 'Til There Was You'. That's Jenny.

The song says, 'There were bells on the hill, but I never heard them ringing. No, I never heard them ringing at all till there was you.' From the first time I met Jenny, I heard the bells ringing. I'm no fool. I locked in on that. I knew a good thing when I saw it. From then on, it was Jenny. Still is. She's the bells ringing. And she's the diplomat in our family.

Let me explain a little more and enlarge on that. The diplomat is always trying to bring out the best in others. Jenny does that in our family. She does that for me. She says it comes out of that central teaching of the philosopher-teacher, Jesus of Nazareth, from long ago. When she explains it, she gets rather philosophical. She can do that almost any time. Let her explain it the way she does."

Jenny looked up a moment, then looked at her audience, opened both hands in an 'let me show you' gesture. "We all face enough challenge in life to force us to reach in and up for the best - for what's really important. But we never do that until we reset the mind so it guides us to use that special ability given to us in our genes - that ability to redirect the mind so it guides us by the winning identity of diplomacy.

We live on recycled energy, you know, like that philosopher-teacher from long ago talked about - that what you plan to give to life comes back into your own - that it becomes a recycling base out of which you have more and more to give, because the best keeps coming back to you. You know, the measure you give is the same one that measures what comes back to you. It's like the Teacher said, 'Give and gifts will be given to you.' We all need that recycled energy that comes out of reaching out to give our best to life, no matter what the challenge. It becomes an energizing power base for living."

When she ended her zestful sharing, Clark pitched in and added, "Like Jenny says, we have so much to give in our time. In spite of that, we meet people who are trying to get without giving. Doesn't work that way. In order to get the best out of life - in order to get a return in maximum benefit, we must give, and do it first. People who are good at diplomacy, work to help others find their best, and in turn, they gets a return on that. Jenny is that kind of outgoing diplomat.

Finding the good in others, and respecting and praising that, is the key to diplomacy that is far above finding the flaws in others and criticizing that. That's not healthy, and that doesn't foster good relations. Children need parents who praise the good in them from age one to whatever age they become. We are their parents. We will always be their parent, and we must always find ways to compliment and praise the good.

So, Jenny is the diplomat in our family, par excellence. Jenny was that kind of person the moment I saw her. She was alive with that kind of outgoing, recycling energy. She radiated it, and still does. And the bells keep ringing. And I am privileged to hear them. That's my song, 'Till there was you.'"

"That's our song," Jenny cut in. "It worked both ways. I heard the bells, too."

Clark paused in a respectful moment as in silent agreement. Then he said, "Let me go back in our story - back to our early days right after my dad died. Mother had died three years earlier. And Jenny can tell it better than I, if she will tell about that day two weeks after Dad's memorial service when we came back out to the farm from the city to spend a week-end out on the apple orchard farm."

Jenny moved forward in her chair and began with both respect and enthusiasm. "We were both deep into our young careers - careers that anybody might have said were ideal for building a great life. And I don't deny that.

We had spent the night out at the farm. I had finished a little put-together breakfast of bananas, prunes, and cheerios and had come out on the porch where Clark had brought his cup of coffee and was just sitting in one of these old rockers.

Silence followed for several moments as we sat there in our own reflective thoughts. That's when Clark said to me, 'Jenny, look up that little road between the apple trees. I once thought that road led out to a world where I could find everything I was looking for. It did, in the sense that it is where I found you and where, in time, both of us found our way into very promising careers. We were happy and successful. But one week-end when we came back out to the farm to visit, I remember what Clark's Dad said. He said, 'Son, this place will be yours some day. Maybe you can find a way to keep it. Just don't sell it without a really good reason. Maybe you can make it a place of dreams, like your mother and I have made it.

There was a long reflective pause before Clark took one last sip of coffee and set his cup down on the floor and looked over at me and said, 'Jenny, how can we make this a place of dreams?' Clark twisted his chair a little more toward mine and just sat there waiting for me to say something. I know he didn't expect the answer I gave. I said, 'Move out here. Bring our dreams with us and make this a place where we can reshape them and let them come alive.'

Clark sat in silence for a long moment. Then when he said that there wasn't a lot of money in the apple business, and the work is long and hard and a big frost can wipe out any year's crop, I said, 'but my teaching can bridge the gaps, and all the while we would be doing what we love and measuring by that, instead of measuring by how big our salaries are, and moving up the ladder.' I think the long silence that followed, really did indicate Clark's surprise at my answer. But move out to the farm is what we did. What our story might have been otherwise, I don't know. All I know is, this is where we replanted our dreams. How we did that, Clark can take the story forward. But, before that, let me say how special it is that you have brought these two old rocking chairs here and asked us to come up and sit in them. Makes it seem like we were both out there on that porch again, when we made that decision years ago. So, Clark could you pick up on the story."

Clark began in a slow and deliberate manner. "It was one of the best quality of life decisions we ever made. We have had some ups and downs and had to live very close at times, but so far, we have never had that big wipe-out frost. And we have raised our children out here and they have loved it. They had the privilege of going to a good school here and learning that measuring by the yardstick of big money is not as good as measuring by happiness and quality of life. Two of our children are in college now and another one headed that way this year, but so far we're keeping the bills paid and consider it a high privilege."

Clark turned a little more toward the banquet audience and continued. "Steve asked us both to read his granddad's books. And, like Dr. Lucas said, when Steve asked him to read Dr. Kelly's books, he said he had already done that. It was the same for us. But

Jenny and I read them again. In his books, Dr. Kelly talks about how location can be incidental to where one lives out life's chosen qualities - that you just must not let place define arrival so much as being on a journey where you just put in your best qualities, and follow what's most important for your dreams. So, it wasn't hard for me to say to Jenny, 'Okay. Let's do it. Let's move to the farm and move our dreams with us, as our place to find what's most important for a good life.'

From then to now we have been testing the qualities of the Big Ten each day. Those words are often a reach beyond our grasp, so we keep on reaching. We try to make them a part of the ways we relate to each other, to our children, and to everyone we meet. It's that simple. When the apple pickers come out to help us, we try to give those qualities a real chance to be a part of our story as we pick apples together. And when Jenny teaches the children at school, that's where she's the diplomat, always trying to bring out the best in others.

Now, I know everybody can't have a farmhouse with front porch rocking chairs, but they can have a set of ten words to guide their dreams to help them discover what is important in their story. And, in our case, Jenny and I have tried to help each other be the best we can be as the guiding markers for our dreams. And we have had the opportunity to be in a partnership with three children, where an overall model for success is to be a learner about life - where what we plan to give to life just keeps on and on being the request we bring to each day, wherever we may live. So the dream lives on. We are still living in our dreams."

The pause was only for a second before Steve said, 'May I ask, how the two of you met, and came to know each other?'

Clark spoke first and said, 'That's easy. And I still cherish that moment. We were on the same college campus. I noticed Jenny sitting on the patio of Waverly Hall where we had our meals. She was sitting in the sunshine, studying, as I passed by on my way to lunch. But I captured that moment in my mind in such a way it stayed with me as I ate lunch and laid out a little plan. When I came back out, as I hoped, Jenny was still there studying. Maybe she wasn't studying so much as just waiting for me. Anyway, I made my daring move. I said, 'Hi. May I join you a moment?'

'You can indeed, especially if you know something about math and can help me figure out something.'

"I moved ahead of that opening and teased, 'What I want to know is why you are still out here waiting for me.'

'Waiting for you? That's not how it is at all. I am studying for a test. And I need to know the material.'

I cut in and said, 'And I need to know you name.' I waited a moment because that was not at all the response she expected. 'It's Jenny Hartsenberg,' she said. 'And your name is?'

'My name is Clark Henderson. But to be honest, I already knew your name. And to be even more openly honest, I have been waiting for a chance to meet you.' With that beginning, we became friends. In fact we became more than friends. We became buddies, just as much as you can be and keep up good grades. We mixed dating and study together. Then came marriage and careers. We were not only in love, but in love with a career, which we launched into after graduation.

Then after the disappointing death of both of my parents, we came back out here for a week-end, and you know that story. We were privileged to take up a place in an ongoing story in which Jenny said of my parents, 'Your mother and dad were two of the most admirable people I have ever known.'"

"And how does all this fit with your faith?" Steve ventured as a leading question.

Clark answered immediately as he shifted back a little more in his rocking chair. "It fits with the faith I grew up on in the World Citizen Church where the teachings of Jesus were not just theories, but practical ways to live and find ways to care.

From time to time I find myself repeating the words of one of the songs we used to sing at church. It was built on the story Jesus told about ninety-nine sheep safely in the fold, but one sheep was missing and the shepherd went out looking for it. It's a story in song about caring. Another song says, 'Others, yes, others. Let this my motto be, that I may live for others.' Caring. Another song repeats the same theme, 'help somebody today, somebody along life's way. Let sorrows be ended, the friendless be friended, help somebody today.'

And those three songs sum up my concepts of what a church ought to be doing - to help us learn how to care - how to build skills and careers and let those become our major channels for caring and for using all the Big Ten qualities. While that may not sound impressive, it is at the heart of a faith that is relevant to our time, and to all time.

That's why it is so right to have an icon, or sculpture, or statuette, whatever you want to call it, of the Master Teacher on the altar of our church. His teachings about caring are at the heart of his story. It is central to who Jesus was, and should be central to who we are trying to be. In that sculpture on the altar, adults and children are standing close by, listening. They are learners, and we are learners. The main business of a church is to help people learn how to make the qualities of the Big Ten real, right in the various channels we use to turn our skills into careers and service. So there are at least five things that are central in my story - home, church, college, marriage to a wonderful partner, and education to build a talent and skills base.

The identity of this church, that my grandparents helped to build, and that my parents were a part of, and to which they brought us three children every Sunday, is built around the Big Ten, even though at that time they hadn't been shaped by Dr. Kelly into the overarching Big Ten Universal Qualities as an identity template. That's why, when Dr. Vernon Lucas advanced the idea that we replace the cross with a statuette of Jesus, I welcomed it.

I spoke in favor of that. It put the premium on learning to live by qualities of life, not theology.

It takes a lot of metaphors to try to tell who Jesus was, but the one that says it best for our digital-molecular age of learning, is Teacher. That's what his disciples and others called him. And they were learners. And that's who we need to be as parents - learners about how to live the best we can. And for Jenny and me, our chosen place to be learners is out here on the apple farm. We try to help each other live out the Big Ten qualities. We tried to teach that to our children.

It goes on. When the plumber comes out to fix the pump, that's when it's our opportunity to live out the Big Ten. And when Jenny meets with the Garden Club, she greets her friends as an opportunity to live out the Big Ten. Out of that overarching framework of identity, we have raised our children and are sending them out into life on their own as learners, and to build their own Big Ten friendships. It works. It releases positive energy into their own self-estimate so they operate out of a higher level of confidence and self-respect. When our children brought their friends home, it was an expanded opportunity for all of us who live out here in the apple orchards and do more than grow apples - it's been our opportunity to care and share.

Now, sooner or later, everybody needs somebody to care about them - to be an understanding and outgoing friend. Living out the Big Ten is the best way to expand caring into a network of qualities that enrich the lives of others. And it can happen anywhere and at any time. People win respect when they give respect away. They win it because they earn it. So, all of us are called to be as big as we can, and care as much as we can, wherever we can. That's what the Teacher was all about and that's what we are trying to be about. And that's at the heart of what we have to say to all of the parents here at the World Citizen Center. That's what makes us Big Ten world citizens.

Jenny and I chose to come back here and take up our story

on the apple tree farm. We could have been successful in the careers we were already in, but we made a choice. We had a chance to be here and see what happened at the World Citizen Church where these leading-edge thinkers dared to place the statuette of the Master Teacher on the altar. I can speak confidently for both of us - we are privileged to be a part of this reach for quality-based living as we take our place here in Alpine on an apple tree farm.

When and where will we make our best contribution to the human story? Who knows? Maybe at home. Maybe in our careers - wherever our journey may lead.

So, one of our high privileges is that of being parents. And we can be better parents when our story is enriched by the guiding qualities of the Big Ten. These can be, both the words we measure by and the words that guide us to be better persons and better parents.

But I've done too much talking. I'll stop and let Jenny talk about all this."

Jenny amusingly said, "Whoever developed that myth that women are the talkers? But really it doesn't matter so much which one of us is speaking the most, what matters is who we are trying to be. And that's what I saw in Clark as we got to know each other, and what made me want to say, 'yes,' when he asked the question about marriage. And I'd say it all over again, today."

When Jenny paused, Steve respectfully entered a new conversation lead. He asked, "How does this crossover into your teaching career here?"

"There is no break between what we try to do here and what I try to do at school. The Big Ten qualities are personality skills. They can be learned and developed. It's one of the things I help children learn at school. First we learn the Big Ten qualities just like we learned the ABC's. We learn them in many fun ways One way is to have each child go to a table and select a card with one of the Big Ten words printed on it, then go to another table where there are lots smaller cards with words on them that have some parallel to the Big Ten. They select one of these that matches the first card they selected card. After that they have fun telling how and why they think they are alike or related. They like that. They never want to stop. It leads into positive conversation among them as students.

They make associations, by contrasts or parallels. We call it CONNECTIONS, and they say, 'Let's play CONNECTIONS.' I tell them not to laugh at strange ideas and associations, but I really don't need to do that. They begin to respect each other's ideas, even if they are far out. So they don't really laugh at another, they laugh with each other.

Out of this they learn to respect each other beyond their differences. They become more tolerant, even diplomatic in that they help each other explain their idea and figure out how or why it fits, or doesn't fit. Out of this they learn to collaborate. They teach each other. It's a marvelous way of learning. It all happens when they work (play) together under the word-tools umbrella of the Big Ten Universal Qualities. It's wonderful.

Actually it is creativity and exploration. It's like research in that it is making new associations and seeing new relationships. It's building skills. For them, it's play. It's like in the Mary Poppins movie, 'a spoon full of sugar makes the medicine go down.' Children can learn the Big Ten qualities at whatever their academic level. Many children who struggle academically, simply delight in learning the personality skills of the Big Ten. They blossom like a flower. They delight in using their newly developed words with friends and their families. They are discovering and building wholesome identity.

These are positive ideas and skills that help them solve some psychological difficulties. These words help them adjust to difficult situations at home and with fellow students. It lowers their defenses and anger. They are friendship building skills at the same time they are building what become, career skills. Teaching these connections is what I enjoy most in my teaching. It's fun helping children develop these healthy emotional relationship words that help them adjust and grow, while they build friendships, respect, and caring. The Big Ten words are wonderful word tools.

No wonder Clark loved the songs they sang at this church when he was growing up here. They were about being caring and helping others. No wonder the members of Grovemont Church were ready to change their name to World Citizen Church as a way of expanding the range of their caring on a broader scale, and then to change the focus of their identity by replacing the cross on the altar with that inspiring statuette of the great Teacher. And no wonder the church was ready to extend their support to creating the World Citizen Center, with its mission defined by the Big Ten Universal Qualities. They had learned how to live by the 'new beginning' words of the Big Ten. Reminds me of the title of Dr. James Kelly's first book, *New Beginnings.* The stories in that book are about identity and who we can become beyond challenges and difficulties, and how failures don't have to be disasters, but learning points where we 'get it' - where endings can be new beginnings. Challenges are opportunities. Children can learn all this. It's fun to teach within this framework of positive thinking defined by the identity markers of the Big Ten.

The Big Ten are dream building words. As they say, 'if you can dream it, you can achieve it.' Dr. Kelly's dream was that these words be taught in all the learning centers of the world. My classroom is one of those centers. The apple tree farm is one of the learning centers of the world for both of us.

I am always pleased to hear Clark say that I am the one who made the bells ring. But then I tell him it was the other way around. So, we've tried to make the bells keep on ringing for each other."

"Jenny and Clark," Steve said, "Thank you every so much for letting us sit on the porch with you. As you shared your wonderful story, we could hear the bells ringing, too! Thank you for sharing your story with us!"

Steve stood as an indication he was bringing their richly rewarding parenting banquets to a close. Turning, and addressing the audience, he said, "Looking back over the past three evenings of our Parenting Conference I want to express my thanks to Dr. Arnetta Segal for helping us to see where we are as a human family in our magnificent universe and on our special planet. I want to thank Dr. Vernon Lucas for bringing us the best of psychology's focus on building our strengths as a way to enrich our living. And tonight we have heard the uplifting story of Clark and Jenny Henderson and the ways the Big Ten Universal Qualities have been the focus of their devotion to each other for a winning life.

Would you join me in applauding each of these outstanding speakers in a very sincere thanks for their guiding and inspiring presentations.

As a long applause turned into silence, Steve said, "What I understand is that just before I close these times together, Clark and Jenny Henderson have something to add. Who wants to speak?" Steve asked, as he sat back down in the rocking chair.

"It will be Jenny," Clark said. "She is our best spokesperson."

Jenny said, "Steve, when you were sitting on our apple orchard farmhouse porch, you showed us your business card. Clark and I liked it! In fact, we liked it enough that we would like to make the back side of our business card like your card. Could we do that, and, if so, could you explain it for us?"

Steve replied with enthusiasm. "You could, indeed put this on your business card! And the best way to explain it is for me to tell you how Granddad explained it to me.

During a reception at the World Future Conference, we were sitting at a table with one of the leaders who had been a part of the beginning of the conference. When Granddad showed him his business card, he looked at it thoughtfully and then said, 'What you need to do is to get these qualities into stories.'

Well, Granddad was already doing that, but he knew what the man said was important. An idea that was already growing in his mind, quickly came into clear focus. He knew he needed to get that listing of words about the future onto the business cards of more people.

When we got back to our room, Granddad said, 'Steve, would you be willing to put this logo-icon with its two contrasting drawings, and its identity words of the Big Ten qualities on your business card? Before you answer, let me describe what I hope is already so obvious that it needs no explanation.

The abstract drawing at the lower left, with its black background and its red entangled dashes seemingly clashing against each other, represents conflict and the struggles that go on in the human journey and within our own personal identity.

The abstract drawing at the upper right, with its light blue background and dark blue dashes moving forward together in concert is equally a metaphorical image, representing unity and our reach for our higher self.

The way to get from one to the other, to get from Conflict to Unity is to choose and live by the words stair-stepped in between - the Big Ten Universal Qualities.

Those ten words are some of the most important words in the progression of our human story! All the people of the world need these guiding identity markers. They are words we can use in our digital, molecular, information age to lead the way to sunrise tomorrows.

The Big Ten qualities are not about the past. They are about the future, even as that future keeps changing! They need to be taught to our children and youth in all learning centers across the world. I just believe that if millions of people would put this logo-icon on their business card it, would help people to define themselves as successful achievers and, in turn, they would want these identity words taught to their children in all kinds of ways."

Granddad finished his explanation by saying, 'That could be a way to help extend my dream that the Big Ten be taught in all the learning centers of the world. Steve, I would be pleased if you would put this logo-icon on your business card, and give them out of as many people as you can, in the hope that millions of others would do the same!'

That's when I said immediately, 'Granddad, I would be highly honored to print this on all my business cards and give them to as many people as I can.'

So, Jenny and Clark, that's the reason I showed my business card to you. I would be very pleased if you would make that same choice and make one side of your business card like mine - like Granddad's.

Jenny responded immediately. "I think I can speak for both of us. As soon as we can, this important logo-icon will be on our business and professional cards. But, may I ask an extended question? Where did the framework identity words of the Big Ten Universal Qualities come from?"

Steve answered in a thoughtful manner. "My first awareness of them was when I heard Granddad use them in his stories about new tomorrows on the farmhouse porch. Even though he may not have known exactly where they came from, he knew they form a very special framework for humanity's identity, gained out of thousands of years of progression in the human story and marking the way to a better future. In that sense, the Big Ten Universal Qualities refocus the collective wisdom of the ages into a new Identity GPS to guide the earth family to a better tomorrow. Even though the Big Ten have grown out of the collective progression of the human journey, they are not about the past, they are about the future! They are about a very important story - our story."

As Steve stood and addressed the audience directly he said, "Now, it's time for me to explain why my business card was placed at each of your place settings. They were placed there as a sample, with the hope that each of you will do what Jenny and Clark will be doing, and put this logo-icon of the journey from Conflict to Unity on your business card, then share them with many people. It's a positive way of living and sharing out of the sunrise perspective of the Big Ten Universal Qualities as world citizens!

So, now, as I announce the ending of our Parenting Conference, I want to announce it, not as an ending, but as an important new beginning, where each of us have a place in the story!

Good Night, and Sunrise Dreams!

SEQUELS: New Tomorrows, Apple Blossom Time, The Future We Ask For, A Place In The Story, Eagles View Mountain, Sunrise Dreams, The New Sacred